The Good Little Ceylonese Girl

A Collection of Short Stories

By

Ashok Ferrey

All characters and situations in The Good Little Ceylonese Girl are fictitious.
There is no intended resemblance to anyone, living or dead.

Cover design by Mahen Perera and Vijay Puravirajan
Pen and ink drawings by Ashok Ferrey

Typeset by The Fontmaster
Printed and bound in Sri Lanka by Samayawardhana

Contents

Acknowledgements

My thanks as always to Madame Ferrey and Sarojini Sinnetamby for their deft fingerwork, and Ranmali de Silva, Jill Macdonald, Ann Scowcroft, Miranthi Huwae and Ray Wijewardene for their invaluable comments.

Last but by no means least I would like to thank Sam Perera and Ameena Hussein, who assisted so ably at the birth of Ashok Ferrey.

For Alexander and Soraya,
The Little Emperor,
The Little Empress.

Fidanzato Fidanzata

It was biting cold up there in the Tuscan hills. I stuck my hands even deeper into the pockets of my Oxfam jacket and continued walking: past the house of the medieval pope that was now a disco, past the little town square, from the Porta Romana at one end to the Porta Fiorentina at the other. Then I walked all the way back.

Joe and I had this arrangement, you see. While Joe entertained I walked. I tell you, by the end of that holiday I had buns of iron, calves of steel. Just as I got back to the Porta Romana a third time the louvred shutters above me burst open.

"He's all yours," she said. "Come and get him."

◎ ◎ ◎

I first met Joe at one of those posh Christ Church dinners – black tie – where you bring guests, usually at your peril because the food is execrable.

"I think," said my invitee rather grandly, "this duck on my plate died of anorexia *quite* a few years back." It wasn't as bad as all that, really. He was Alfred Dunhill's grandson. What did he know about ducks?

There was a commotion as Joe, who was the person on my other side, climbed up onto the table knocking over a wine glass or two. When this Hall was built in the sixteenth century it was the largest room in the kingdom. To command it you have to have the sort of voice to carry up to the rafters of its splendid hammer beam ceiling.

"I would like you all to join me, if you will, in singing a little song," he boomed.

"Three jelly fish...." And three hundred voices sang after him,

"Three jelly fish ...."
"Sitting in a dish...."
"Sitting in a dish...."

Joe was my best friend at Oxford, though what he saw in me I really couldn't tell you. I suppose I was his conscience, his alter ego, his good angel. Not that Joe was dark or evil or menacing. On the contrary he was good at everything. A little too good for his own good, if you know what I mean.

"I'm leaving this place," he said after only four weeks of term. "I'm off to Italy for higher studies."

"What sort of higher studies?" I asked, perplexed.

"A course of higher studies in women."

"I didn't know they had courses like that."

"Oh, don't you believe it," he replied. "In Italy I hear there are splendid openings for keen students like me. Only one thing though. Do I mean higher studies, or do I mean lower studies?"

I took the train down to Italy as soon as term ended, to Monte San Savino high up there in the Tuscan hills. Sri Lankans didn't need visas those days but at the border they inspected my sachets of cloves, cardamoms and thunapaha with deep suspicion.

"For curry," I explained. They didn't understand but they let me through anyway. You leave Sri Lanka with the firm conviction you'll be happy if you never see another curry as long as you live, but at some point in your career your convictions falter, and before you know it you're knee deep in curry. You're back to your roots really; ginger as well as turmeric.

When I stepped off the train at Monte the whole station stopped and stared. They had never seen a black man before. It was the only time in my life I was able to appreciate the meaning of the phrase *time stood still*. I felt like God on the Seventh Day.

I lugged my suitcase up the hill to the little flat by the Porta Romana where Joe lived, above Signora Sirra his landlady. The good Signora's husband had died during the War and nothing very exciting had happened to her since then, and your beard could grow grey before she finished her war stories and let you go. The trick was to sneak past the open doorway of her flat where she sat knitting, permanently in black. It wasn't easy I tell you.

"Good thing you're here!" said Joe when I arrived panting at his door. "I'm inundated with work. I find I've cornered the market in *fidanzatas*."

Before we go any further let me explain this thing about *fidanzatas* and *fidanzatos*.

In Italy those days – much like Colombo these days – you lived at home till marriage, death and sometimes even beyond. So what was an eighteen year old girl to do to have herself a little fun? She went out and got herself engaged of course, to the first thing in trousers that came along. She became fidanzata. That way she could step out at seven every evening, leaving her moustachioed Mamma growling indoors. After all, if your fidanzato couldn't protect your virtue from others, who could?

The funny thing is, your fidanzato probably got engaged for the very same reason. It gave *him* exposure to a whole lot of girls – usually other people's fidanzatas – that he would normally not have access to as a single man.

Monte at that time had a whole flock of these free-range fidanzatas, all out to have a good time, fluffing and preening their feathers. They took one look at Joe and decided to a man (or do I mean bird?) to take up his offer of English lessons. Joe always has this effect on women. I can't think why.

"Some nights I'm so tired I can't sleep," he complained.

"Oh?" I replied, a little icily.

Of course Joe didn't restrict himself to Monte alone. In his little butu-butu Fiat we ranged far and wide over those Tuscan hills. There was Anna at Anghiari. There was Teresa at San Sepolcro. Of her he said, "It's a good thing my tastes are so catholic, her arms are so short."

"Good thing," I sighed, "how noble!"

Then there was Rosanna the kitchen maid at Castle Gargonza, ancient and wooded and Gothic. (The castle, not Rosanna). She was like a tiger with shoulder length chestnut hair. I spotted the beginnings of a moustache on her cute upper lip. Trouble. I told Joe so.

He blinked his baby blue eyes at me. "When I require your advice on women, I'll ask for it," he said. Rosanna cooked us dinner at two o'clock one morning in the dungeon kitchens of the castle. Dante himself had eaten there some six hundred odd years back.

"I don't think they bothered to clean up after he left," Joe whispered.

Rosanna threw two dry chillies and six cloves of garlic into half an inch of bubbling olive oil. Then she tipped in a bowl of cold cooked spaghetti and enriched it with shavings of parmesan.

Delicious. I still cook this sometimes. And I think of her.

Rosanna was not one bit interested in learning English, so Joe made her the standard offer: first lesson free. That was usually enough.

In between his strenuous English lessons Joe took me on cultural outings, "since your Oxford education has left you so painfully deficient in the finer points of life." He took me to Palazzuolo to listen to the padrone's accent – "the finest in all Italy, the purest music." He showed me frescoes by Giotto. He bought me wine at the Palazzo Antinori and ice creams at Perché No? I am ashamed to say very little of this remains in the mind, except maybe the wine.

It was Joe's idea to throw the party, towards the end of my holiday, a sort of graduation for all his English students. There were twenty odd fidanzatos and fidanzatas, a whole brood, clucking and quarrelling among themselves. It was rare to get them all under one roof, and more than a few feathers were being ruffled. If you ask me, the mood that night was quite fowl.

I cooked them curry. Chicken, of course. When in doubt, give them curry, has always been my motto.

Early on, the party split into two groups. Those who had enjoyed Joe's novel teaching methods, and those who were about to. The hads and the had nots, so to speak. The former were led by Paola, a large doe-eyed girl with a treacherous smile. I remember her well because the first day I met her she asked me:

"Are you black all over?"

"Do you want to check?" I replied. Or would have if only I'd had the nerve. She was furious because her position as favourite was about to be usurped by Luisa who led the other group. The two sides began singing songs at each other, with a sort of violently cordial competitiveness.

Nobody touched the chicken.

"*Troppo piccante, troppo piccante,*" they all said. I retired to the kitchen with a few disgruntled fidanzatos, where we moodily picked at chicken bits from the aluminium pot with a common fork.

I couldn't tell you which side won the competition. My Italian wasn't good enough to understand the violence of those songs, but even I could appreciate the rolls of thunder in the music, the jagged streaks of lightning across the sky, the oncoming storm.

◎ ◎ ◎

The louvred shutters above me burst open.

"He's all yours," Rosanna said, "come and get him."

I passed her on the stairs coming down. To tell the truth I was a little nervous and for once I wished Signora Sirra was there to interrupt us. She wasn't. Rosanna gave a little laugh.

"You'd better warn your friend," she said, "not to mess with girls like me."

She tucked a stray curl behind her ears. "In fact we were all talking in the village the other day, it's a great pity *you* weren't the one teaching us English."

And I was so dumb back then I didn't even know what she meant by that.

The flat was a tsunami zone. Joe sat in the middle of the destruction dabbing a cut on his lip with a piece of bog paper.

"You'd better watch out," I warned him. "They're all turning against you."

"*Really*?"

I could see the thought of a pack of hot angry women mobbing him was doing interesting things to various parts of his brain.

"You're getting a really bad name for yourself. Rosanna is only the start."

He gave me a smile that would have melted snow off the Dolomites. It left me unmoved. I had seen him practising it in the mirror many times. I just looked at him. I could have said: "I told you so, I knew the moustache was trouble."

But I didn't.

Joe was quite simply one of the most gifted guys I've ever known: here he was, throwing it all away. I was sad for him, I was angry for him.

In fact you could say I was black all over.

"You'll stay a few more days to help me clear up, won't you?" he pleaded.

I half considered sending my tutor a cable: "Unable travel, blood on tracks."

But I didn't.

It must have been the only occasion in my entire Oxford career that I got back well in time for start of term.

Dust

In the two week run-up to Sri Lankan elections, over eighty churches were attacked. Many were vandalised and looted, some were torched. Then elections were over and so was this sudden gush of violence. For the moment at least, the taps were turned off.

Father Cruz was dusting the pews again. Mrs. Jayakody watched him in some distress. She stood at the back of the church, hardly daring to breathe in case he should see her. One part of her wanted to intervene, to help out. The other part said no, stand firm. He's the one who's got himself into this mess, now let's see him get out of it.

But Father Cruz was in a world of his own. Every once in a while he looked up at the window high in the tower through which light streamed down, and watched the little golden motes of dust swirling all around him. He looked like an angel in a *quattrocento* picture, about to float up to heaven in a dusty whirlwind of gold.

He may look like an angel, Mrs. Jayakody thought, but in real life he was proving to be quite a little devil. That last row with the parish council had been the worst.

"How can you possibly expect us to organise a cleaning rota for this place when you insist on keeping the church doors open all hours?" she asked him, in her capacity as President. "Don't you realize, Father, that drug addicts and dogs, tramps and peanut-sellers all come in when it's too hot outside?" She was firm with him almost to the point of cruelty.

But he just sat there with a vacant look on his face. Finally he said quietly, "I'll do it myself. I'll clean the church."

The Church Ladies tittered. Really, it was too absurd! Father Cruz was barely able to keep himself clean, so how was he going to manage a whole church? In fact Father Cruz was beginning to look quite like one of those tramps they were trying so hard to keep out. He hardly bothered to shave, and there were lavish growths of grey sprouting from his nostrils and ears that he never bothered to trim. This subject alone occupied a fair amount of their time when the Church Ladies met every Thursday morning. Only Doreen de Mel, who was partial to a bit of hair on a man, was in favour.

She was outvoted seven to one.

Father Cruz moved slowly from one row to the next. He noticed there was woodworm in the last two rows. The pews would have to be replaced. It was not that the parish was poor; there were more than enough people willing to donate new pews, new floors, new everything. Even stained glass for the windows in the tower. Up to now he had said to each of them: Thank you for your kind offer, but this parish has more pressing needs. He explained to them there were children who needed school uniforms, there were homeless people who had to be fed. But rich parishioners were strangely unwilling to give to such insubstantial causes. They preferred to put their money where they could see it, or more to the point where others could see it: in a shiny granite floor or a blazing stained glass window, preferably with a plaque affixed bearing their name. Father Cruz politely showed them the door, explaining that if they weren't happy for him to spend the money as he saw fit, they were better off taking it elsewhere.

This they frequently did. His congregation was dwindling: he was losing numbers to younger, shinier churches, where you dressed to kill and danced in the aisles, and vied with other members to see who could contribute most money in the most spectacularly public fashion.

Father Cruz finished another row and decided to have a little rest. His eyes took in the shabby pews, the tired paintwork, the birds nesting in the rafters. When I'm gone, he thought. When I'm gone they can do it all up, not before. But the Church Ladies were getting impatient. Only last week a bird had crapped on Doreen de Mel's perm during High Mass.

The political parties were squaring up for yet another election. Father Cruz wondered wearily if the same violent events would recur, if policemen would again have to be stationed at the church doors. He had had great arguments with his friend Abey about the violence.

"It's the will of the people," Abey said spreading his arms wide. "It's all part of the culling process, part of Nature. When a tree grows too fast, when a population increases too suddenly, Nature deals with it in her own inimitable way."

Father Cruz had become really angry then. Islam and Buddhism are the fastest growing religions in the West, he wanted to say. Are they then to be culled too? But he thought of the bombs going off in Europe and the sudden violence that had then been unleashed against peaceful Muslims, and he kept quiet.

His church had escaped last time. He knew the reason: it was not a glamorous church. There was nothing there worth taking, not even the souls of the few nondescripts who worshipped there. But he also knew that even if the mob had razed it all to the ground, the almost palpable devotion of the countless numbers who prayed there over the centuries would hang in the air, and the very motes of dust would be charged with all that holiness. That was how sacred places were created: a thousand years later, long after the buildings were gone, people would be turning up, tying scraps of cloth to the trees, leaving behind offerings of fruit and flowers, not really knowing why......

There was a sudden sneeze behind him, and Father Cruz jumped guiltily in his seat. Mrs. Jayakody stood before him, blowing her nose vigorously into a white, over-size handkerchief.

"It's the dust, Father, the dust."

He looked at her for a moment. "The dust," he said. "It is indeed the dust."

◊ ◊ ◊

Nobody really knew when the church had been built. Most likely during British times, but the fabric had been butchered in the name of modernization so often in the intervening centuries that what you saw now was a poor shadow of what it once must have been. The last outrage had occurred in the Sixties when the then parish priest, flush with the weekly takings, had brought in a prominent architect to usher the church into modern times, to provide a space more conducive to the liberal free-thinking spirit of the age.

His answer was to do away with the stained glass and remove the marble balusters of the altar-rail. The carved wooden altarpiece was replaced by a large off-white hemispherical shape with the sacrament at its centre placed in a smaller, golden hemisphere. The whole thing resembled a woman's breast, which was probably the architect's intention, though he perhaps never bargained for the mirth and merriment it afforded young toughs of the neighbourhood who stood at the back during Mass.

One of the first things Father Cruz did was to drag the old wooden altarpiece back into place. The marble balusters had been dispersed a long time ago; he still came across the odd one here and there in the houses of the poor when he went to visit the sick.

◊   ◊   ◊

It was Tuesday, the feast-day of St. Anthony to whom the church was dedicated. Father Cruz stood in the doorway, duster in hand, looking out nervously. He was the elderly host whose dinner guests have started to arrive before he's quite finished laying the table.

People of all religions came on Tuesday: they lit candles, they breathed in the dust, they went away. But there was something in the air that brought them back, week after week.

Row upon row of smartly-dressed beggars lined the drive. It was the one day of the week their lunch-packet was assured. Inside, politicians mingled on equal terms with peanut-sellers. It was usually quite hard to tell them apart.

Father Cruz was waiting for his friend Abey. He heard the familiar hum and rattle of his brown diesel Pajero before he saw him. It was rumoured that Abey had been born a Catholic; but he could be seen in temples on Poya Days, mosques on Fridays, churches on Sundays. He visited St. Anthony's on Tuesdays.

"What actually are you?" Father Cruz asked him.

Abey spread out his hands in an all-embracing ecumenical gesture. "I'm everything and I'm nothing," he explained. "I'm a man of the people."

But he was genuinely fond of the old priest. They retired to the priest's quarters at the back of the church for their weekly glass of arrack. From the verandah they watched the steady stream of people.

"Don't you get tired of all this, Father?"

Father Cruz longed to tell him: I'm so tired I can hardly stand. I should have retired years ago. But every year I beg them, please let me stay a little longer, please. Because I know that when I go, it won't just be the priest that goes. A lot more will change.

"Isn't it time the church moved on, Father? Aren't you cramping their style a little bit?" It was almost as if Abey was reading his mind.

"To tell you the truth, the thought of weeding flower beds at Ampitiya in my old age doesn't attract me a great deal. The thought of living up in the hills, among other old priests. . ." His voice tailed off hopelessly. But even as it did, he knew he wasn't telling the whole truth: it was not the thought of where he was going that made him unhappy, it was the thought of what he was leaving behind.

Father Cruz had always felt that any place of worship should be like a mirror held up to the people who prayed there. His mirror happened to be speckled and dark with age, the silvering worn off in places, so you couldn't see properly; you didn't always understand what you were looking at. But sometimes, if you were lucky, you saw beyond what was actually there: you saw more. The trouble these days was that people were impatient. They wanted shiny new mirrors that showed up everything at a glance. They wanted to turn up the lights, stand in front in all their nakedness and say: Look at me, this is me, this is me in all my glory! They were not willing to submit to the will of a grander design, more obscure, more beautiful. So they smashed up the old glass. And then the old magic was gone, and they didn't realize; and it was too late anyhow.

There was also this: an old mirror did not incite greed and envy in others. There was less danger of others smashing it for you.

Father Cruz had read somewhere of the tourist who had visited St.Mark's in Venice, and looking at the sloping floors and thousand-year-old mosaics, had said: "What this place needs is a level floor and a *darned* good coat of whitewash."

He was brought back to the present by the sound of Abey's voice.

"At least take a holiday, Father. Do you have any brothers and sisters?"

Father Cruz had a younger sister, married and living in Ja Ela.

"Go and visit them, Father. The end of next month would be good."

"Why the end of next month?"

Abey opened his eyes wide. "Why ever not? It's as good a time as any."

◊   ◊   ◊

The Church Ladies went in deputation to see the Archbishop. They were led, naturally, by Anoja Samarapala, whose nephew ran a pizzeria at the Vatican. His kukul mus pizza was the delight of many a Cardinal (she said). No one really knew whether the Holy Father had as yet had a taste.

After a great many cancelled and re-scheduled appointments they managed to corner the Archbishop in the gardens of the Palace where he was trying to have a nap on a swing seat. It was two o'clock in the afternoon. It was so hot there wasn't even a cat in sight.

"He's got to go, Your Grace," they said. "He's too old, he's making a right mess of things. We need a change."

"He's got to go," agreed the Archbishop wearily. He almost added, "So do you."

But he had got the message loud and clear. Barely a fortnight passed before the new recruit arrived. He was plump and personable, his name was Father Pinto, and when you saw his quick-humoured flashing eyes you knew that before long there would be dancing in the aisles. The ladies put it to him that it was imperative to keep the doors of the church closed in between services, and really, wasn't it a shame it was dedicated to St. Anthony, because every Tuesday the whole world and his mother paid a visit? A Christian church must be for Christians alone, mustn't it?

Father Cruz shook his head muttering to himself, but it was no longer up to him. His days were numbered. He wandered about aimlessly with his duster. The guests had arrived and dinner wasn't even cooked.

◊ ◊ ◊

As it happened, his sister in Ja Ela couldn't have him at the end of the following month. It was the time of her son's O'levels, and she couldn't afford to have any disturbance in the house.

So Father Cruz was actually praying in church when they came.

It was a still night, the church doors were open. It was some time before he sensed anything; he could hardly hear over the rasp of his uneven breath. He turned his rheumatic neck as far as it would go, and saw the black hooded figures standing silently at the back. His heart seemed to break its bounds, to hurl itself at the walls of his ribcage with a violence he hardly knew he possessed. As always, it was his body he was unsure of. Please God, he prayed, don't let me shame you in your own House.

There was a slight undulation at the edge of his vision, a cat's breath of air on the back of his neck, and he knew they were walking towards him. His hands began to shake. He gripped the pew tightly to stop them. Don't be afraid, he whispered to himself, they're only human, after all. They've only come to break the glass.

The Church Ladies discovered him in a sea of rubble next morning. He was gasping for breath but by some miracle he was still alive. Father Pinto laid him down gently and loosened his collar. There was dust everywhere and the sunlight streamed down on his body, turning the motes of dust to gold.

"The church will be rebuilt, of course," said Mrs. Jayakody firmly. It was almost as if she was trying to convince herself. "It will be bigger and better than ever. And perhaps we might consider dedicating it to a different saint?"

"Is there a Saint Doreen?" wondered Doreen de Mel.

Father Cruz's breath was becoming more irregular. Father Pinto knelt down and spoke gently into his ear.

"Think carefully, Father. Who were these people? Did you recognize any of them?" But Father Cruz shook his head. Had he heard the familiar hum and rattle? He couldn't be sure, it was all so much like a dream.

His dying voice struggled to come back to the surface one last time. "The motes," he seemed to be saying, "the motes......"

"Notes?" asked Mrs. Jayakody joyously, "Notes?"

She turned to her fellow parishioners. Her eyes were moist. "Ladies! I do believe he's hearing the celestial choir!"

Love in the Tsunami

They found themselves washed up together on
the beach by the mighty wave, that mighty wave of
NGO's and newspapermen, well-wishers and ghouls
that swirled into the country in the wake of the
Boxing Day Tsunami.

"A broom for you," said the woman. Veena
noticed the fair, thick hair that hung over the
woman's face, her very dark eyebrows that seemed
almost painted on.

Interesting, she thought. They worked side by
side for a while, cleaning the beach. The woman,
Veena noticed, worked better than any man, pulling
heavy chunks of debris out of the way, throwing back
her head every once in a while and laughing silently at
some private unshared joke. It made a change
anyway from the sort of glum, *I'm-here-with-the-
tsunami* type of face people were beginning to
cultivate around then. A channel of sweat flowed
over the woman's shoulder blades, drenching her

short khaki tee-shirt, flowing down like a great river between the well formed globes of her buttocks. The locals watched astounded, standing about in silence. It didn't seem to have occurred to them to lend a hand.

Help us out here, Veena wanted to say. It's your beach after all.

When the sheer shock of the disaster had worn off and the roads were once more passable, Veena had driven south with nothing more in mind than a vague desire to help out.

"Leave all that to the professionals," Mrs Patel had cautioned her. "There are people better qualified than you. You just stick to your designing."

"You mean there are people out there with PhD's in Tsunami Studies?" Veena shot back. She ignored her mother as she did most times and headed down; and here she was, broom in hand.

The woman said: "My name is Deborah, but you can call me Debs." And by the end of the day Veena was well and truly smitten.

Veena's grandfather was Gujerati, one of a small band of buccaneers that had landed in Colombo before World War II in search of trade. Conditions were so good he had immediately called his kinsmen over. First they established themselves in teakwood and steel; then came paper and gemstones. Now there were garments and electronics.

They settled in Kotahena and Grandpass – the industrial heart of the capital adjacent to the port, with its warehouses, its whining saw-mills, its thundering container traffic. They formed a small community, discreet, powerful and immensely wealthy, the almost invisible twill running through the fabric of Sri Lankan society. Nevertheless, they kept unshakeably to their own customs and beliefs. For their *dussehra* festival in the month before New Year, Gujjus all over India gathered at the crossroads of their villages: they formed concentric circles, men and women, presenting sticks to each other in a courtly and ceremonial dance. And the Gujjus of Colombo did likewise: gathering together on the furry carpet of the Intercontinental Ballroom, clashing their sticks in a frenzy of goodwill.

But Veena had rather gone and spoilt it all by wanting to become a designer. Bad form. Awkward too, since she was an only child destined to inherit.

"Go to America," her father said. "Design all you want." Then come back and take over the family business, he wanted to add. America was where you went to work out all your youthful aberrations, get them out of your system, purge yourself. You came back cleansed, hopefully, and ready for your dose of Real Life.

But it hadn't quite worked out that way. Virtually all Veena could remember about America was the boat she and her friends crewed that belonged to Mies Van der Rohe's grandson. She remembered it through a Pimms-fuelled alcoholic haze: maybe that, not the wind, was what had made the boat go so fast.

Once back she continued to design. First there was the wickedly cantilevered stainless steel staircase leading up to the room Haramanis occupied over the garage, Haramanis their live-in domestic. It was probably too good even for a Los Angeles Art Gallery. Unfortunately it was sadly below par for Haramanis, who cursed loudly as he skittered down its dew-laden steps every morning. Then there were the teak and titanium kitchen cupboards she designed for her mother, on their spindly metal legs. (*Wretched girl*, said Mrs. Patel, how on earth does she expect me to clean underneath?)

But Veena was not unhappy being back. One of the joys of living in Colombo was that you lived many lives simultaneously, in different time zones. For a start there was your home life, which had basically remained unchanged since the eighteenth century. This was in stark contrast to your work life, which had zoomed off well into the twenty-first. And if that wasn't enough, there was the life out there on the streets, stuck somewhere back in the middle of the twentieth. Nowhere exemplified this better than Kotahena, with its throbbing arteries, its teeming in-your-face ugliness. It gave an excitement, an added depth to her designs not easy to achieve abroad. She had come to understand it wasn't the staircase alone that was beautiful: it was the staircase with Haramanis on it, cussing roundly in the eighteenth century manner. That juxtaposition of old and new was immensely satisfying, like the single cracked-gilt chair in the all-white minimalist room.

Every weekend the tsunami workers came up to Colombo. Mostly young, mostly good-looking, they worked hard, they played hard. Wine sales soared. Restaurants boomed. Colombo took on the tinselled honky tonk glamour of a frontier town during gold rush.

Veena and Debs met up at Barefoot for the jazz. That normally sublime walled garden was packed with so many foreign bodies it was a positive epidemic. You had to look hard to spot the odd – very odd – native brown face. They pushed their way to a corner table with their pints, and there was such a racket going on it was easy to get personal.

Debs worked for an American NGO which concentrated on the world's trouble spots. It was extremely well funded and could move man and machinery around the world with incredible speed.

"I have to be prepared to go wherever I am needed at a moment's notice," she said putting her beautifully square-cut, man-size hands over Veena's, looking into her eyes with the urgent intensity of a soldier about to go off to war. Veena could see how well she wore her battered, wounded weaknesses on the outside, with careless ease, unashamed. But inside was that silent laughing confidence, that assured strength so often lacking in Sri Lankan men. At least the ones they were forever trying to fix *her* up with.

The latest candidate on this list was Kamal, son of Mrs. Ratnam who took her early morning walks with Mrs. Patel. Mrs. Ratnam stood for property development with a capital P. Colombo had recently broken out in a rash of tower blocks, Ratnam Court, Ratnam Towers, Ratnam Residencies. There were even *Ratnam Cottages* for the less fortunate.

"One day," sighed Mrs. Ratnam pointing to various carbuncles in the middle distance, "one day all this will be Kamal's." She made it sound as if this was a matter of some regret.

Veena's mother quickened her pace, saying nothing.

Veena was brought back to the present by the sound of Debs's voice.

"It's the truth we are all after," she was saying. "When I find it, I just go get it." She looked at Veena: "If I really want something I go straight for it, the direct route."

Veena shifted uncomfortably in her seat.

"The shortest distance between two points: the straight line. Don't you agree?"

But Veena wanted to ask in reply: "What if the truth is a moving target, so your route to it becomes a series of zigzags? Isn't that then the shortest distance?" But she didn't want to spoil the mood. Instead she continued looking into the eyes of her new found friend, deep as seas.

"Come with me," Debs said. "Come with me to Darfur, come with me to Aceh. You're wasted here."

"First you'd better come with *me*," Veena replied. "Come up next weekend and meet my mother."

○ ○ ○

They spent the rest of that week texting each other uncontrollably. Veena took to shutting herself up in the bedroom straight after dinner so she could get in a full three hours of texting before she fell back exhausted on the bed. God, that Debs woman never slept! Even at two in the morning sometimes the phone rang. Veena's thumb ached from the sheer physical exertion of this homotextual relationship.

She came down to breakfast, face bloated and bleary eyed.

"These early nights are killing me," she complained.

"My daughter is designing something *big*," said Mrs. Patel to Mrs. Ratnam.

"Something to do with tsunami. She's up all hours."

"She's looking rather like a tsunami victim herself," said Mrs. Ratnam, a little acidly.

Debs was coming to dinner that Saturday night, driving up from the south straight after work. Early morning found Veena in the kitchen.

"To what do we owe this honour?" asked Mrs. Patel.

"I'm cooking dinner for Debs."

Mrs. Patel had to sit down, the shock was so great.

"I'm making Gujerati food."

Mrs. Patel covered her face with her hand. She began to heave uncontrollably.

"Oh Ma, stop being so dramatic. You'll like her. She's such an easy-going person. I thought I'd make *kachori*."

"Kachori?" The word escaped Mrs. Patel like an ill wind.

"Oh Ma, go practise the harmonium or something. Go clash a few sticks. And don't come back till I'm finished."

But by the end of the afternoon Veena could understand what her mother meant about Gujerati food. She was exhausted. She felt like she had done the work of the entire cast and crew of *Guess Who's Coming To Dinner?*

So when the bell rang at six she half expected Sidney Poitier on the doorstep. It was Mrs. Ratnam with her grandson Raju.

"Your mother invited us to dinner."

They pushed past her into the living room, sitting down, making themselves at home, and Raju began the exhaustive business of taking the house apart.

Veena looked at them. "Come in, take a seat, make yourselves at home," she said. "Don't mind *me*."

Veena couldn't stand children, particularly Raju. In a Hindu household this sentiment was about as popular as a steak dinner.

She smiled sweetly at him. "Go on," she said, "play with those fragile crystal ornaments. They're my mother's favourite."

When Debs arrived Veena showed her the staircase, then the kitchen.

"You're wasted," Debs repeated. "You should be designing in LA."

Veena remembered wandering around Beverly Hills during her time in the US, looking at houses greedily, absorbing every detail. She had decided to walk, something quite unheard of, quite Un-American. Horrors! Nobody walked in LA! There were beautiful brick sidewalks bordering perfect patches of grass, planted with discreet sign boards that read *armed response*. But nobody had come running out at her, guns blazing, rather to her disappointment.

"They thought you were the cleaning lady," her friends remarked, and Veena was secretly quite pleased.

She traversed acre upon acre of silently manicured perfection under a cloudless blue sky. Then, turning a corner, she saw a house being remodelled: and she realized with a shock it was all plywood and chicken-wire, no bricks or mortar anywhere, the sort of construction even a tsunami victim back home would have turned his nose up at. The beauty was, literally, skin deep.

Nothing had brought home more clearly to her the difference between design and decoration,

architecture and pastiche. Veena had felt strangely let
down by America after that.

Debs was explaining to the dinner guests that
work was not going well down south. They were
being obstructed at every turn by bureaucracy. Some
of the homeless people were even asking for money to
help rebuild their *own* houses. Others preferred to
stand around and watch. It wasn't easy figuring out
their mind-set.

Veena's Gujju dishes were arranged on the lazy
Susan around which they all sat. Raju was expert at
spinning the disc away from you just when you
needed it to stay put, so you reached out to spear a
forkful of mango and ended up with a pickled
aubergine in your face.

Veena and Debs had polished off the major part
of a bottle of red and were playing footsie under the
table. Mrs. Ratnam watched in horrified fascination,
a snake mesmerized by two charmers.

A phone rang somewhere in the house. Debs
patted her pocket and looked around.

"It's mine," she said. "Now where did I leave it?"

Mrs. Patel came in from the kitchen with a plate
of parathas in one hand and a mobile in the other.
She put the plate down and handed Debs the mobile.

"Crank caller for you," she said. "Some woman
in LA. *Says she's your wife!*"

They sat in rigid silence straining to hear every
word. Debs was murmuring endearments in the
kitchen where she had vanished with the phone. Then
she came back in. She put her beautiful square-cut

hands on the table and leant forward, beaming at them. She might have been at a board meeting.

"Shit happens," she said. Then she left.

Veena felt as if a large block of concrete had fallen on her head from a great height. Mrs. Ratnam sat transfixed, refusing all further food. (The halwa lay uneaten in the kitchen.) Really this was better than any dessert.

Raju had the last word as he left with his grandmother.

"I wonder," he mused, "do I say Auntie Debs? Or do I say Uncle Debs?"

And now, complete radio silence. Veena waited and waited for the call that never came, the call that might hopefully explain that it was all some ghastly mistake. Her now disused thumb throbbed with the ache of textual frustration. On the bright side she was now getting her full eight hours a night. Even Mrs. Ratnam had to admit Veena had got her face back, and was looking quite lovely, *really*.

And then the following Friday, when Veena had just about given up all hope, a message came. "Meet me at Barefoot, same time, same table." When she arrived there was a woman in kaftan and mirrored glasses sitting at their table drinking a pot of Earl Grey, so she hovered till Debs arrived.

"Married!" she exclaimed when they were out of earshot. "*Married.*"

Debs put up her hand as if to ward off these blows. "It was a mistake. Anyway, it's not as if it's recognized in many places in the world."

"What does that matter?" Veena asked tearfully. "You made a choice. Where does that leave me?"

"Listen to me." Debs gripped Veena's arm tight. "What was right for me there, at that time, is not necessarily what's right for us here and now. I have many different lives, Aceh, Darfur, LA. It's very complicated. I can't be expected to reconcile them all, so don't ask me. The reality for us is what is here, what is now."

"So what you see is what you get," said Veena. She added in a small voice, "And what you don't see is what you don't get." She thought of the houses in Beverly Hills.

"Don't you think," said Debs fiercely, "that what we have together, you and me, is the truth?"

"And a month, a year later, when you get tired, or the job moves you on, will the truth move also? And what do I do then, sit around like a war bride cherishing fond memories of the white hero who showed me the way?"

She had gone too far with that word *white*, though, and she was sorry the moment she said it. There was a small contained explosion.

"Oh you make me sick, the whole bloody lot of you!" Debs shouted. "You stand about open-mouthed for all this tsunami aid to get your life back. You can't do a thing for yourself, not even sweep a goddamned beach! Then when we take the trouble to tell you what needs to be done, the right thing, you curl up and get all complicated. It's intellectual laziness. You just can't be bothered to think things through. If you only did you'd realize the way to the truth is usually the obvious way, the short cut."

But Veena's mind was still on what Debs had said earlier. "We're all forced to lead many lives simultaneously," she countered gently. "We do it out of necessity, not choice. We don't make a virtue of it."

But Debs wasn't ready to listen. She got up. "I'm asking you one last time, are you in, or are you out?"

Veena slowly shook her head. To tell the truth, she didn't really know what she wanted, whether she wanted in or out. She knew for sure the way for her wasn't up the lift to the penthouse of Ratnam Towers. But it occurred to her that there was some distance from the point at which she now was, to where the truth might lie. And the shortest route between them wasn't necessarily a straight line.

Vitamin V

"I'm going to a large old house in Somerset for the weekend. I'll wear my oldest clothes, I'll go riding in the afternoons and I'll positively refuse to shave."

They do not believe me of course. They are perfect in every way where I work but their perfection does not encompass old clothes or smelly horses. For you see, I work in Hell. I understand there are many branches all over the world, but mine runs beneath one of London's most exclusive streets. They keep telling me how lucky I am to have this job: contrary to popular opinion it is very difficult to get into Hell, and if the customers are exclusive, the staff are, well, perfect. Except for me of course.

Confidentially, between you and me, I know the only reason I got this job was because they needed someone of my race. They like to think they stock everything down there, and they get a bit embarrassed when members ask for something they don't have. . .

We set off in the dying afternoon, my friends and I, for Somerset, and true to my word I have left my razor far behind in London. The sky is a deep orange and the thought of an empty country house somewhere out there in the warm dusk fills me with a deep sense of contentment: it is as if it has always been expecting me, quiet and resigned, like a father awaiting his prodigal son. It is good to be back up here, where life is chipped and cracked, and flawed and real. For perfection is only an illusion, though they like to think otherwise in Hell: perhaps only I know better, because I have to clean it up every morning before the customers arrive. I look at my friends: she has silver blond hair and a complexion like fresh milk; he is dark and French. They may not be perfect but to me their smiles are worth more than all the beauty you find in Hell.

It is dark and chilly down in Somerset, but he is a good cook, my friend, and after some hot soup and steak my stomach is full, the fire is warm, and I begin to nod. And when I go to bed that night, for once I am not panicked. They are in the next room. All I have to do is shout. . .

"Turn around," Alan says. I suppose I should call him Satan because he owns Hell but that doesn't sound very friendly. "You're a bit on the thin side aren't you?" I should like to tell him I haven't had a square meal the past two days but I don't, because I figure that might ruin my chances. Anyway I get the job, *lucky old me.*

"Report to Sam at seven tomorrow morning," Alan says. Sam is thirty-five but does not look a day over nineteen. There isn't a wrinkle on his face and even his voice sounds young. They may not have the secret of eternal youth down here in Hell but they make damn sure they give their customers that impression. The work is hard and the hours long, but I don't complain because I've learnt the hard way that work in any form is good. I sing old-fashioned songs from the Merry Widow while I scrub the floors and though he won't admit it, Sam likes to listen when I sing.

Keep your mind intact while you're shovelling all this shit, I've told myself, and you'll be all right. I suppose I am honestly a little frightened that I'll end up like the retired fishmonger who can never quite get the smell off his hands however much soap and water he uses, but as long as there is a little part of you they can't quite reach, you are safe. I believe that in this line of work it is quite easy to protect your soul, though very few will agree with me. Just as very few will agree when I say that people do not come to Hell to be taken care of: they have their families back home for that. Instead they want to be pried apart and ripped open, their innermost existence laid bare. They want to be shaken up and wrung out like a wet cloth, and hung out in the sun to dry. And when you have done this to them they are eternally grateful to you, because in some funny way you have made it easier for them to bear their innermost sins by exposing them. Of course they will never give a second thought to doing the same to you, so busy are they in their orgy of self-revelation. And therein lies your safety.

I think I am quite good at my job – the customers like me, and my colleagues are a bit in awe: "Where do you get all your energy from?" Sam has asked me on more than one occasion. I think he would rather I slowed down to the pace of my fellow workers, lest I burn myself out before I come to terms with my existence, but that is the last thing I want. When you are shovelling shit you don't want to come to terms with it: you want to get the hell out before it gets to you.

But it is tiring work all the same. And when I come back up to the real world I want what nobody in Hell can give me: I want to be taken care of. How pleasant it is to close your eyes and lie back in a warm current of water, to be swayed this way and that, gently but firmly, like waves lapping at a boat in some deserted cove. And though they will never know it, my friends do exactly that for me. Their strength lies in their goodness and innocence, and though it may not be possible, I should like them to stay that way forever. . .

When I open my eyes the room is flooded with sunshine. I must have forgotten to draw the curtains last night. I poke my head out and the air is fresh and slightly damp and there is a blue haze over the

Mendip hills. Far away a dog is barking. I don't know the time because I have left my watch behind too, but it must be early. My friends are still sleeping so I pad downstairs and out into the conservatory. I sit in a garden chair in my pyjamas, breathing in great gulps of geranium-scented air. If this is not happiness I don't know what is. But there is no time to waste. My friends have woken up and we are going riding. The last time I rode was at school, a stubborn brute who threw me off frequently, adding injury to insult finally by turning round and biting me in the leg.

My horse is called Maggie and she leans to the right. It's hot up there in the hills but there are many woods where the sun only penetrates in shafts of light, stabbing and dazzling the squirrels who scuttle from tree to tree in the smoky interior. When we reach the green plateau at the top it is time to gallop. When Maggie wants to go you can't stop her and off we go. I can hear my friends urging their horses on close behind and Maggie, who can't bear coming second, flies like the wind. I hang on for dear life, one hand on the saddle, the other desperately shuffling the reins to make them shorter.

We reach the top and collapse in laughter. After the horses have cooled off it is time to go down. But my friends have not finished for the day yet. After returning the horses to the stables they decide to climb Cheddar Gorge. . .

In Hell the lighting is subdued as is proper for a place of self-worship, and there is a constant tinkling of music, usually Abba. To this day I can't hear Abba without having a violent reaction. As you can imagine it is quite hot, so for work we wear shorts and trainers. Even so, my colleagues manage to look smart, while I only manage to look silly, because my shorts are tatty and my trainers have great holes in them. They call it the *small island look* and it is the source of much mirth.

Whenever I get a spare moment I sneak into the kitchen and stuff myself with toasted ham and cheese sandwiches, which is about all the kitchen is capable of producing.

"You're always eating," Latifah wrinkles her nose at me.

"That's where he gets his energy from, isn't that right Jonathan?" Siddiq winks and nudges me in the ribs. Latifah is not her real name of course. Neither is Siddiq his, nor Jonathan mine. In Hell we each have a first name, a convenient tag.

"I'm singing in church on Sunday. Will you come?" Latifah asks. I shake my head. "I told you. I'm off to Somerset." Latifah is nearly six feet tall and has long elegant limbs, the most supple I have ever seen. She is much in demand in the nightclubs where she dances, and also here in Hell, but on Sundays she leads the choir in her local church.

"But I'll be there," Siddiq reminds her. "Blimey, number forty-eight was a difficult one," he continues. "She kept asking me all sorts of questions and all I could do was smile. I think she wanted to save me from myself." Siddiq is perhaps the coolest specimen of them all. But he opens his mouth and the illusion is shattered. He comes from Bangladesh via the East End. Sam has told him to keep his mouth firmly shut when he is working.

"Jonathan, throw that sandwich away. You're late for number twelve."

Sam comes in and breaks up the party.

"Me? But I've just done one."

"Never mind, she specially asked for you." He grins wickedly. "All ten stone of you." As I go out he pats me on the head. "Give her a rough time," he says, "she likes it that way." I know that already from experience, and that's what's worrying me. . .

As usual my friends choose the most difficult way up Cheddar Gorge, a steep almost vertical path cut into the rock. There are trees growing out of the rock face and you have to hold on to what you can to pull yourself up. My friends race ahead and I bring up the rear rather reluctantly, in my trainers with the great holes in them. Every time I look over my shoulder the view is more magnificent.

Gasping for breath we reach the top in time to see the sun set over a metallic white sea. Up here there is still light, but down below the road stretches like a dirty brown ribbon into the darkness.

"Come on," she says, "time to go home." But which way? We have wandered so far across the top it is impossible to find the way we came up. Almost every way leads down so we plunge recklessly through the copper-coloured bracken. At least my friends plunge, laughing and giggling. I slide as cautiously as I can on my backside. Funny sort of way to be taken care of, really, but after being a sadist all week it's fun being a masochist for a change. The undergrowth is turning purple in the twilight as we skate down the final stretch of gravel at the bottom.

Back home she bakes scones for us and we eat them hot with mountains of whipped cream and homemade raspberry jam.

"We're staying Sunday, aren't we?" they ask each other, and my heart sinks for early Monday morning I'm due back in Hell.

"I think we should go back," I say weakly.

"Monday's a bank holiday," they remind me. But Hell works on bank holidays. It works seven days a week, twenty-four hours a day. No rest for the wicked.

All the same I finish my bath long before they do and nip downstairs. I pick up the hall phone praying they won't hear the click on the extension upstairs.

"Hello, can I speak to Sam please?"

"Sam's off duty. Jean-Luc here. Can I help you?"

"I hope so. My name's Jonathan, I work there. I've come down to Somerset for the weekend and the car has broken down. We're going to try and get it fixed but you know what it's like in the country. I may be a bit late Monday morning. I hope that's OK?"

I can hear the chuckle at the other end of the phone. "I'll leave Sam the message." He doesn't believe me but I don't have a chance to improve on my excuse because I can hear the bath water running out.

By the time they come down I've cooked dinner – fish in cream and cardamoms – a North Indian dish. She is wearing a black dress with a touch of gold at the throat and I don't think she has ever looked lovelier. And when I go to sleep that night I feel tired, more tired than I ever felt after a day in Hell. It's good to work, of course. Even better to enjoy the company of your friends. . .

The marble entrance to Hell is somewhat larger and more plush than the eye of a needle, and all the rich and famous of London gather there. Frankly, I never saw an uglier lot.

There is something honest about the ugliness of real people. But when the wrinkles are stretched and the sagging bits taped up they begin to lose all humanity, taking on a sub-terranean sort of look.

As for the beauty you find down there, it is refined and manicured to a too perfect standard. My colleagues move with a grace too feline to be human, too calculated to be animal. To watch them congregate in that kitchen is to watch a room full of prima ballerinas, each the dying swan. An embarrassment of riches.

But I'm afraid to say there is one thing common to all of us, a common missing element so to speak in our makeup; a debilitating weakness that binds us to each other and keeps us united, like victims of some esoteric and unfashionable disease: charming children of the Third World, we're hopelessly deficient in the one vitamin so essential to a fulfilled and nourishing life above ground. Vitamin V, I call it. *V for visa.*

But we don't talk about it. We see the signs of affliction in each other's eyes, we are afraid.

I have tried hard to dislike my fellow workers but each day it gets more difficult. They have adopted me as their mascot and each tells me minor, inconsequential secrets he would be shy of telling the others. Who, after all, is afraid of revealing himself to his pet dog? With Latifah it's her religion; with Siddiq his insecurity about his accent, and Sam, even Sam has his love of schmaltzy music. The only one who remains aloof is Marek. There are pictures of him plastered all over this town smiling as if he hasn't a care in the world, but in the flesh his features are as hard as granite, never relaxing for a moment. He lives quite close to me and the other day we shared a bus home. Just before he got off at his stop he pointed to a window high up with two faces at it, both sandy haired, both freckled.

"My old woman and my kid," he said. Six words that have since made it a little bit easier to like him.

Their trust in me makes me want to reciprocate, and each day I pray: Oh God, if only I could. But to love somebody is to give of yourself to them. What you give you can never take back: what they possess of you will always give them a hold over you. This phase of my life has to be lived in layers, each a separate skin, and when the time comes as it must to slough off this particular layer, I don't want to feel as if I am chopping a limb off because there are people out there who possess a piece of me. . .

It is Sunday morning and the church bells are ringing. I am in the conservatory as usual with a small tray of water-colours and a jam jar of water. I can feel the fingers of sunshine massaging my back and the layers of liquid green flow down the paper and merge with the layers of yellow and blue. If only life could always be like this. One day, I vow, one day.

There is a Saxon church in the village and although it belongs to a religion none of us follow we decide to go. The church is cool and dark inside, and deserted, for we have missed the midday service, thank God. And when we come out, I put my arms around them and say, "We'll travel back Monday, it's settled." They look at each other secretly and smile. To them there was never any question.

After lunch we pack a fishing rod and two jam jars – one full of water, one full of worms – and set off for the river. There is a solitary cow in the next field who seems to want to join us. In fact she is getting quite chatty over the fence. The fact that we have caught nothing the whole afternoon is of no consequence. It has been a good excuse to lie in the long tall summer grass making daisy chains.

And when we get back in the evening, surprise, surprise, they are showing the Merry Widow on the box, and I think of all those floors I shall not be scrubbing tomorrow, and wonder with despair who am I trying to kid by saying I can manage to keep the layers separate. It is always like this with my friends: the very comfort and happiness I draw from them during these rare weekends serve also to rot the strength of mind I need to possess if I am to survive in Hell. It is my fault, not theirs.

Perhaps I am doomed to live the rest of my life oscillating between contented indolence and disciplined fanaticism, never entirely happy in either state because of the memory of the other.

That night I have bad dreams, and when we set off next morning it is in silence. As we drive up the motorway I long to reach out from the back seat and touch my two friends, like a pilgrim who touches the holy shrine for the last time, knowing full well that the memory of that touch is all that he has to take back with him.

But I can't: I feel paralysed, and though it is sunny outside there is a chill creeping up my legs.

Maleeshya

"What I need," said Maleeshya flicking her copious red curls over the back of the chair, "now what I need, is a really good death."

"We could all do with that, dear," said Mrs. Bibile her assistant.

"No, what I mean is a brilliant death, a magnificent death. I can see it all now," she said, as her vision grew, " horizontal bands of lapis lazuli and gold... rather like the inside of Tutankhamun's lavatory, really... and the subject sitting on the throne all gold-plated and stiff in his rigor mortis. There you are, that's your front cover!"

"Hah!" said Mrs.Bibile. Mrs Bibile was a woman of traditional build, with a bun and a great line in nylon saris. Her glassy black eyes reflected little zigzag sparks of wickedness. She had vim, vigour and what-have-you: in short, everything you could wish for in a personal assistant. She also had attitude.

If there was one thing Maleeshya couldn't stand it was attitude.

Maleeshya was the editor of Shuh!! Magazine, so named to differentiate it from its ugly European elder sister, Shah!! Magazine. Their formats, logos and layout were virtually identical, but there the similarities ended. The Sri Lankan version was pungent, tropical, laced with odd but strangely exciting ingredients – rather like the local curry, really – so different from the blandly parboiled milkfood content of its rival. It was filled to bursting with natty *natukottai chettiars* in heirloom jewellery and jolly mudalali millionaires, embattled beauty queens who had lost more than their crown at competition, and canny, country-bred kumarihamys with sons fattening nicely for market.

There was, however, one basic requirement before you were allowed to appear: you had to agree to undergo Maleeshya's knife. And rather like those carved vegetables so beloved of the Hilton buffet on a Saturday night, you ended up leaner and meaner, and frequently unrecognizable. Maleeshya was the chef, you were her legume: so it was not you that appeared in the magazine but her vision of you; and if you were unrecognizable it was only because you had in the pictures what you never had in real life. You had edge.

The funny thing was, what she turned you into was what you actually became, for that short time the edition was current. The Word made Flesh, so to speak; or Life imitating Art imitating Life. Because Maleeshya was the artist and real life her raw material.

The phone rang. Looking at the display with a slight groan Maleeshya answered it. "Yes Mrs. Iddamalgoda... No I did get all your previous messages. The truth is we're overdosed on weddings this month, but I'll see what I can do...Five daughters? That's a record surely! No I didn't mean to be flippant...Sorry, I know, I know... look, if you're there this afternoon at 4.30 I'll try to make it. Bye!"

The fact of the matter was, Maleeshya was bored! bored! bored! She was tired of weddings, she was tired of christenings. She was tired of overdesigned interiors and underdesigned underwear shows. What Colombo actually needed was a damned good funeral. Trouble was, people were so inconsiderate these days: they died and got buried before you could say Shuh!! That old Mrs. Ganhewa last week – really it was so selfish! – they had buried her first and notified people afterwards. If you were going to be like that, frankly, you were better off dead.

"What we need," said Maleeshya, "is to be notified at least a week in advance that a demise is about to occur, so it gives us time to order the flowers, rehearse the music, plan the guest list.

"What we need," she said looking at her assistant sharply, "is for somebody to get off their butt and go check out the hospitals: for a list of the grateful dead, the grateful dying. The very nearly, dearly departed. They need to appeal to the Apollo,

liase with the Oasis, scour the Nawaloka. Depart at
once to Durdans, Durdans, Durdans!

For a traditionally built woman Mrs. Bibile
could shift with surprising speed. And she did.

❀ ❀ ❀

It was said by people who knew, that Maleeshya
wielded more real power than the President herself.
But unlike the President her power was absolute: she
never forgave, she never forgot. Or hardly ever. Oh,
and she had the power to make you appear and
disappear.

There had been that famous case last year of the
Sumitra Sisters with whom she had had a major
falling out over some fairly grave matter like a double-
booked hair appointment or the poaching of a
pedicurist. They were cut out of the magazine
entirely, and that meant out of life itself. In these days
of digital enhancing and erasing it was the easiest
thing to do: they simply failed to appear at any event.
So that people who had actually met and chatted to
them at these events said to them afterwards, where
were you at so-and-so's, I didn't see you in the
pictures? The Sumitra Sisters had disappeared from
the Colombo social scene like wizards in a digital
puff of smoke.

About a year after the falling out there appeared
the nose of one sister and the be-ringed hand of the
other on either side of a rising young starlet, and a

reconciliation of sorts was effected. But the Sumitra Sisters *never appeared full-frontally again*. Except in real life, of course, and as anyone knows that doesn't count.

I Shuh!! therefore I am, as Descartes might have said if he were living in Colombo.

❊   ❊   ❊

"Mrs. Iddamalgoda, I will cover your daughter's wedding on one condition."

"Yes?" said Mrs. Iddamalgoda a little apprehensively.

"I'll do it if she gets married in black."

"What!" The cry rang out sharp against the polished stone floors of Mrs. Iddamalgoda's architect designed residence.

"Well maybe you can have the bridegroom in white," said Maleeshya relenting a little. She shifted uncomfortably. The architect had designed a set of award-winning chairs for the living room. Nobody sat in them for long.

Mrs. Iddamalgoda was taking the news badly. It had been difficult enough to get the bridegroom's people to agree to the marriage in the first place. The idea of black might drive them away entirely. On the other hand an appearance in Shuh!! was virtually essential to clear the backlog of daughters.

Mrs. Iddamalgoda thought back with a little shiver to the call she had made from hospital to her husband when the youngest was born.

"Not another bloody girl" he roared, crashing the phone down. He was not present at the birth of any of his children: no Sri Lankan father ever is, if he can possibly help it.

Quite a few are not even present at conception.

Just then, as if to remind her, the reflections of the two youngest girls shimmered across the granite as they crossed the hall on silently slippered feet.

"This season," Maleeshya said encouragingly, "all the chandeliers in Murano are coloured black."

"My daughter is *not* a chandelier," Mrs. Iddamalgoda replied with great patience.

"She will be by the time I've finished with her," muttered Maleeshya, but the other did not hear, sitting as she was on the far side of that interesting, award-winning coffee table.

Later that day Maleeshya and her assistant met up at their ritzy headquarters on Flower Road.

Mrs.Bibile said: "I do believe I've found you your candidate. Mr. Arishtabotale Pereira."

"Arishta who?"

"You remember, the author. Shortlisted for the Gratiaen a couple of years back. We made him change his name, poor sod, to make it more reader-friendly."

"Did we? How rude!"

"Ashok Ferrey."

"Oh yes. I vaguely remember now. Little fellow. Grey hair, grey eyes. Grey teeth."

"He's at the Apollo with a heart condition. Not expected to last the week."

"He'd damn well better last the night," threatened Maleeshya. "I have a wedding and fashion show to get through before I deal with *him*."

And so the day passed. It got dark and the traffic eased up a little, and a figure stepped out of the offices. It peered at the world, this way and that, through luminous grey eyes, and shook its curls. Then it teetered off to the aubergine BMW parked at the curb. Gone was the boring daytime business suit. In its place boots, thigh-high, and miniskirt, sky-high. The editor of Shuh!! Magazine was about to hit town.

❀ ❀ ❀

With the remains of last night's margaritas swirling around inside a painfully splitting head Maleeshya ventured deep into Ferrey country, into the heartlands of Dambalapitiya.

She negotiated the aubergine BMW onto Galle Road and immediately got stuck behind a group of students in starched white, marching three abreast in the slow lane. She edged past them with difficulty, letting her window down with a swoosh.

"Why walk on the pavement when there's a perfectly good road?" she asked. (They might have replied, "Are you kidding? Don't you know Colombo pavements are strictly for cars only?") But they saw the BMW, the red curls, and they began to simper and preen, thinking it was their lucky day. Maleeshya raised the window back up and beamed at them through it.

"Morons!" she said.

They waved back delightedly.

Further on in the fast lane she swerved to avoid an emaciated hermit-like figure with a wicker basket of vegetables on his head, tacking and veering across the road in a whirl of his own. The hermit leapt lightly into the third dimension, his vegetables raining down on motorists in a multicoloured monsoon shower. Slowing briefly to make sure he was unharmed she sped on, leaving vegetables to purée under the wheels of oncoming cars. A pity, she thought, the vegetables looked so fresh; even if the man was a little ashen.

Then onwards into the steaming green heart of Dambalapitiya Junction, where the natives were out in force and everything displayed on the pavements for sale, plastic bowls, rubber toys, glass vases, grandmothers. Surprisingly, nobody seemed to be buying anything, not even grandmothers. The whole exercise looked like some vast Newtonian experiment in perpetual motion, with no beginning and no end. Turning off the main road Maleeshya plunged up a rutted lane. But once inside the doors of the *Hacienda Ferrey* she realized she was wrong because most of Dambalapitiya seemed to be in here too, with glass vases and multicoloured bowls on every available surface. It wasn't going to be easy creating Living Art from this little lot.

"I've come about the funeral arrangements, Madam," she said to the rather stout figure that answered the door. (She called everyone madam till they were proved otherwise.)

There was a loud wail as the other burst into raucous tears. Maleeshya proffered a somewhat used tissue and waited. Perhaps a kitsch funeral, she decided. An unadorned coffin of plain mangowood planks painted a chemical pink. A chorus of jaya mangala girls in frothy cerise tulle.

"What do you mean funeral?" Mrs. Ferrey had recovered from her tears. She sounded quite belligerent.

Maleeshya didn't want to drag Mrs. Bibile into it. That might have made things really ugly. Instead she said vaguely: "Oh people at the office, you know . . . . your husband won't last the week they said. . ."

There was another loud wail. Maleeshya surreptitiously looked at her watch. She had forty minutes till her next appointment. Really, this woman was impossible.

"Listen Mrs. Ferrey," Maleeshya said urgently. "Your husband was a great man. I should know, I *created* him. 'Don't give up the day job,' I said to him when he was short-listed. (And he never did, thank God!) He was plain Arishtabotale Pereira back then. But you know as well as I do, writers are poor creatures at the best of times, quite unable to look after themselves, let alone us. . ." She patted her red curls. "Just think what a five page spread in Shuh!! will do for you when he's gone. *You need never work again!*"

She hit the Galle Road half an hour late for her next appointment, the contract signed and safely tucked away in her favourite handbag, the one with cherries all over. She called the office.

"Bibile," she said, "what do you consider more kitsch: orange gladioli or pink anthuriums?"

❈ ❈ ❈

Mrs. Iddamalgoda called three times in the ensuing days. Would a deep portwine colour do, she asked, because the bridegroom's mother particularly objected to black?

"Give her wine," said Maleeshya, "Oh let her have her wine. Only don't tell her, we might have to push her off the magazine pages entirely; this funeral thing seems to be really taking off."

The phone lines around Colombo were buzzing. They rang red hot at the Ferrey household :

"Can I speak to the Widow Ferrey, please?"

The reply was silence, followed by a loud wail.

❈ ❈ ❈

There were scraps of white flag fluttering all the way up the rutted lane. Banks of orange gladioli and pink anthurium, and a curiously Gothic purple croton lined the drive.

Maleeshya was covering all bases. Inside, the multicoloured bowls were in place, the kitschness complete. Maleeshya paced up and down in a fever of impatience. The Shuh!! spies posted at the Apollo had rung suddenly to say the body was on its way. It was too soon, it was the day of the Iddamalgoda wedding. But Mrs. Iddamalgoda had been outraged when it was suggested at the last minute she move her date back, and had refused.

"Damn that woman!" said Maleeshya. "If she's not careful I'll rub her out entirely."

There was no need to damn the author. He was sure to be in eternal damnation already. Inside the house were more flowers. The English Writers Uncooperative had sent a daring arrangement of bamboo and banana blossom. There was a single cryptic rose from Shuh!! Magazine's Bride of the Month, the colour of blood. With it a card which read, *Better dead than wed*. The Iddamalgoda girls had clubbed together and sent a wreath of poison ivy.

It was not a good night for marrying or burying. It was the night of the Architect's Ball and Maleeshya had a date with the American Ambassador. She would be hard pushed to wriggle into a ballgown by ten. Suddenly there was a noise outside and an aged green Datsun clattered up the drive. It coordinated prettily with the crotons but was so old, alas, it was not really *shuh-worthy*.

A grey haired man got out. He saw Maleeshya and immediately sucked in his stomach.

"*Ko* hearse?" she asked him.

The man looked behind him to see if there was a cortege following. There wasn't.

"And who are you?" asked Maleeshya switching languages.

The man gave her a charming smile. He had slightly discoloured teeth. "I'm the author," he replied proudly.

"You can't be! You're dead."

He straightened up. (There was not much straightening to do, he was quite short.)

"Madam," he said with some gravity, "I fear that reports of my death are greatly exaggerated."

At this moment Mrs. Ferrey came round from the back of the car where she had been unloading tiffin carriers and enema tubes and porcelain pee-bottles, all the detritus of a happy hospital stay.

"Isn't it wonderful?" she beamed. "He's alive and well!"

"No, it isn't," said Maleeshya. She could be quite short with people, though these people were short enough already. "The flowers are paid for, the caterers are setting up the mala batha on the back verandah. You *promised* me a funeral." The Ferreys looked blank.

"I reserved five pages for you. Now what will I do with them? Not even Mrs. Iddamalgoda can stretch to five pages." There was silence. "Let's not forget, I created you. The least you can do is to let me destroy you." There was more silence. Then the author raised his hand. He began hopping from one foot to the other like the fat boy at the front of the class who always gets the answer right. "May I make a suggestion? It's Ashok Ferrey you created. So why not bury *him* today? And I can go back to being Arishtabotale Pereira." There was a little squeal of delight from Mrs. Ferrey. She began bouncing up and down like a cartoon wife. "I never liked you as Ashok! Never, Never, Never! My dearest darling Arish." She began smothering him with kisses.

Maleeshya resisted the urge to vomit into the nearest multicoloured receptacle.

Instead she gave a sickly smile.

"Does this mean," asked the author, "I need never write again?"

"Perhaps a series from beyond the grave?" suggested Maleeshya helpfully.

Then a thought occurred to the ex-author.

"There's no body," he said.

"So let's make it a closed-coffin affair."

"But there are no people here. I mean, my fans naturally won't come because, you see, I'm not dead, am I? They'll be celebrating my return quietly, in the privacy of their homes, drinking arrack-and-ginger beer on their back verandahs. . ." He was lost for a minute in his little, literary world of Ashok-Ferrey-fandom, his mouth puckered in complacence. He looked at that moment singularly unattractive.

"Oh don't you worry," Maleeshya cut in. "There'll be people here all right. A hundred of Colombo's finest. The crème, so to speak, of the bloody crème." She looked at his puzzled face. "Oh they're not coming for you, my dear, or your book. They're coming for me and my pictures. Face the facts Ferrey, it was never about you or your book, was it? It was only ever about me and my pictures."

Maleeshya looked around at the food, the flowers, the hideously chic banquet chairs covered in pink and tied back with gilt bows: all evidence of her Living Art. She felt supremely satisfied. It had been a close call, but as ever, Shuh!! Magazine had triumphed.

But the evening wasn't over yet. She began punching numbers on her mobile.

"Mrs. Iddamalgoda? Hold your horses – oops! – I mean daughters. I'm on my way!"

The Ola! Ola! Club

Every day on his way back from the insurance company Ramal walked past the Gloucester Arms.

"Thursday night jazz," the board said. And every Thursday streams of very good-looking Continental girls milled about outside, in tight white jeans and fluffy tops. Ramal longed to join them: he could hear the rusty sawing of the musical instruments inside and smell the hot food and wine. Instead he walked home to Ambrose House. Ramal had a single room in lodgings, with a single bed and a small Baby Belling cooker on which he scrambled eggs most nights.

The other inhabitants of Ambrose House – and there were many, and not a few Sri Lankan – preferred to boil their dhal and grind their sambals. He never caught sight of any of them, they were always much too quick: they flew ahead of him silently down the carpeted corridors, wafted along on

warm currents of dry fish and roasted chilli. Some
nights you could almost hear the furtive fizz of
Elephant House ginger beer from behind the closed
plywood doors.

Ambrose House was a charitable institution run
by Mrs. Amor, a tall woman with straggling blond
locks. She rattled a large bunch of keys as she walked
about, like a sort of amiable gaoler.

"We like to make our foreign guests feel
welcome," she said. Every weekend   Mrs. Amor
could be found at Portobello market, selling war
medals from a barrow at the wrong end of the road,
right down at the bottom, among the overblown
cauliflowers and squashy bananas with black patches
on them. Ramal came across her one Saturday
afternoon. He smiled at her, but she looked straight
through him.

Ramal worked in a steel and glass palace a short
bus ride from home, in a vast open plan office. There
was an island of four desks facing each other, three
girls and he. The girls were English and therefore
quite out of his league. The job wasn't arduous,
logging in personal details of various city magnates
onto the computer, so the actuaries upstairs could
work out how many millions to insure their lives for.
There was usually a running commentary from the
girls.

"Cor, I don't half fancy this Mr. Willis here.
Trouble is, see, he's got this prostate. Now what I
want to know is this. If I show him a good time, will
he be up to it on the night, d'you think?"

"And why should you care? You don't fancy him, do you, you only fancy his millions."

"You're just jealous, you are. Bitch."

Ramal worked silently through this cross-talk. The girls watched him with polite disinterest: they filed their nails while he filed their data.

One Thursday evening Ramal plucked up courage and walked into the Gloucester Arms, into a comforting aura of hot pie seasoned through with the winey strains of jazz. He paid his two pounds ninety and went upstairs but could only find one spare seat, at a table for three. "Is anyone sitting here?" he asked tentatively.

"Yes," they smiled, "you are."

"I'm Javier," said the man, "this is Rafaela."

Ramal couldn't help noticing they were almost impossibly good-looking, with features so precise they might have been cut out of a picture-book by a child of nine.

"I'm Ramal," he said. They began talking to each other in some foreign language. The musicians finished sharpening their rusty instruments and suddenly, dramatically, the jazz began.

The girl turned to him. "Settle our argument," she said. "Are you Iranian? I think you're Iranian. But my husband thinks you're from Bangladesh." Her eyes were like those little bits of clear green glass you sometimes see stuck in the eyes of ancient Greek statues.

Ramal shivered.

"I'm from Sri Lanka, actually." He looked at them in confusion. "I didn't realize you were a couple. I mean you look so alike I thought you were brother and sister."

She smiled at her husband with a look of secret complicity. "Everybody thinks that. It's part of our disguise, part of our protection."

The music cut in on them but they were more interested in him. What did he do?

Where did he live? Why was he here?

He began to tell them. And what little there was! The contents of a child's toy cupboard laid painfully bare for all the world to see. Under normal circumstances he would have been ashamed at the sheer poverty of it all, but there was something about the wine in the air, the rasping acid jazz, that made him brave. And anyway, they were well padded against the bare bones of someone else's existence – "Daddy bought us a mews in Elvaston Place when we got married," she said – and perhaps the thought of all that property sat in them like the remains of some heavy meal long after it has been eaten.

He tried to explain about the country he had left behind, the choices he'd had to make. They registered the mildest concern: his worries were like little flat stones skimming lightly across the surface of their well-being. They were interested in an intellectual sort of way. Perhaps, he thought, they want to improve me, make me their good deed for the week, maybe this month is Save-A-Sri-Lankan month. But he wasn't bitter: he wasn't that sort of person.

It was only natural after all to want to save your fellow man, and the rich were particularly keen on that sort of thing. But he wanted to explain to them very gently that though Elvaston Place was no more than a quarter mile up the road from where he lived, the actual distance, spiritual and temporal, between his room and their house was far, far greater than the distance between Colombo and Kilinochchi. He was, in reality, a long way below their reach. But it wasn't in his place to point this out: nobody likes their good intentions thwarted, least of all the rich. Sometimes, he thought sadly, the poor know too damned much for their own good.

So instead he turned to face the music. A George Melly lookalike was singing:

"You need a little sugar, in your bowl,

You need a little hot-dog, in your roll……."

They took his arm excitedly. "We have plans for you!" they said. "Come with us to Madrid for the weekend, we'll pay your ticket – only 59.99 on British Midland, not much – we want to take you to the *Ola! Ola! Club*. We'll have fun, won't we, and it won't cost you a thing!"

He looked at their shining eyes, their expectant lips. And for a moment his happiness rose absurdly, like a scrap of paper surging forward on the tide of their goodwill. But life was beckoning to him from behind the closed doors of Ambrose House: it shook its straggling locks at him, and rattled its war medals, and in the background you could almost hear the hushed fizz of the ginger beer bottles.

"I don't know," he said uncertainly.

"*I* know, let's all have a drink." She pulled out a very crumpled twenty pound note from her handbag. "Javier let's get a whole bottle." She turned to Ramal.

"Go and give him a hand."

On their way to the bar he asked, "Have you been married long?"

Javier looked at him one long, cool moment. He too had the same green-glass eyes.

"A year. I love her, you know what I mean?"

They fought their way to the counter, and in spite of the crush the barmaid materialized in front of them instantly, like some sort of vinous miracle.

"Hi Precious! We'll need a bottle of your finest Rioja." Javier smiled at her. When she had gone to fetch it, he turned to Ramal : "That's Claire. Now what I like about Claire is she has nice firm jugs, you know what I mean?"

When the bottle and glasses arrived he said to Ramal, "Take these back to Raf, there's a good boy. I need to have a word with Claire, won't be a moment now," and he winked.

But Ramal never saw him again the rest of the evening.

"He's talking to her again, isn't he?" Rafaela said when he returned, and together they polished off the bottle in moody silence. So much so, the stranger who had taken Javier's seat leant over to them and said, "Cheer up you two, married life can't be as bad as all that!"

At the end of the evening Ramal gallantly offered to walk her home, but the clear sharp air outside had done something to her senses, and she said abruptly, "Take me to your room. I want to see where you live."

It wasn't far. They negotiated the locked doors of Ambrose House and the labyrinthine corridors in silence. She took in the overglossed cream woodchip walls and the frayed carpet of the room with the practised eye of the very rich, and he cheered up at the thought that even if it had been all Baccarat and Chippendale it probably still wouldn't have made the grade. But they were in the single bed now, their clothes all over the floor, and he thought, it really doesn't matter anyhow, does it, because nobody looks particularly rich or poor in the dark.

He caressed her hair, her face, her lips. Then his fingers encountered her eyelashes and he realized with a shock they were wet. He sat up on his elbow to look at her. The little bits of green glass were cracked and weeping.

"I can't," she whispered. "I love him, you see."

And so, he thought with almost triumphant despair, a good woman!

The price of a good woman they said was above rubies. As she snuggled up to him and went easily to sleep he felt strangely exalted, lying awake in that bare, poor room.

In the morning when he awoke she was gone. He had overslept, he was late for work, breakfast was not a possibility. Grabbing his overcoat he ran for the bus, hurling himself on with suicidal abandon. As he wedged himself in between two very young, very fat people, he felt a strange crackling all around him.

He reached the steel and glass palace that was his office, and as he ran through the revolving doors of the entrance he began to pull out from his coat pockets dozens of crumpled notes, ten pounds, twenty pounds, all denominations, even Spanish pesetas.

Running across the great marble atrium with the sunlight pouring down on him he began to laugh.

The Indians are Coming!

The Indians flew in like a flock of wild birds early Monday morning.

"I'm Sandesh Bhattcharya," said the director. "And you can call me Batty."

"Suranjeet Pimbalavaner," said the producer, "just call me Pimply."

"I will, I will," I said peering.

"And you are?"

"I'm Avanka Wanninayake," I said.

"Call me Wanky," I added helpfully.

Before we go any further let me explain to you how I got into this curious business of acting. All I ever wanted in life, you see, was a house with long white columns and endless verandahs.

I was lucky: I got my wish early on, at the tender age of twenty-six. But what you get is never quite what you imagine. Nobody told me then about the leaking roof, or the defective drainage, or the subsidence in the servants quarters. Nobody told me that an old house is merely a hole in the ground into which you pour money.

So then I started hiring it out for films. The house by now was infested with rats, bats, cats and kids. Also a Wife. So half a hundred extra film crew lurking in the bushes wasn't going to make that much difference. One day I came back from work – a film was in progress – and the director gave me an odd look.

"I want a policeman," he said. "I'm desperate."

"You have a thing for the armed forces, do you?" I asked him tactfully.

He looked blank for a second.

"No, I mean for the film."

So they sent me to Wardrobe to get measured up and dressed, they gave me my two lines to learn, and half an hour later I was on. The less said about that particular performance the better; but one thing led to another, and here I am now, an actor, dear boy, an actor!

I met Sanju later that afternoon in the low-rent gym we both frequent. (I've been using it so long there's nothing older there than me; except possibly the floor carpet.)

Nobody bothers to dress up, you go as you are; and one of the nice things about the place is that it is remarkably free of gold-smugglers, pimps and drug pushers, who tend to favour the bigger, more air-conditioned establishments up the road at the five stars.

"They're shooting at home," I said.

"I know," Sanju replied. "I'm in tomorrow's scenes."

Sanju is one of those meaty specimens who features regularly on our small screen, sitting decoratively in the far corner of many a shot wearing a loincloth and playing the flute. Alas he doesn't get to speak many lines; but he does get lots of work. I swear one of these days he'll get his big break, acting the CEO or something, sitting behind a posh desk in shirt and tie. And loincloth.

I, on the other hand get to play the intellectual parts. Like policemen. The high point of my brilliant career came of course when I had to lead two thousand people at Maradana Railway Station in a big budget extravaganza. I got up on the podium, shook my fist at the camera, and shouted:

"Gandhi-ji's in the bath!"

And two thousand people roared after me, "Gandhi-ji's in the bath!" (The actual words were *Gandhi-ji zindabad!* but I found my version more effective.) This five minute scene took three days to film, naturally. Well, they released the film at Toronto the other day, and I found they had cut me out almost completely. Though there's this very good shot of the back of my head so I mustn't complain.

Actually if truth be told, Sanju is a clerk in an insurance company and I am the assistant librarian to an assistant librarian; but we don't discuss these less savoury aspects of our lives down the gym, because we wouldn't then be able to patronize our fellow members, those less fortunate creatures lower down the food chain. Like our friend Yacoub, for instance, who does all this fancy, poncy catwalk stuff for Odel and the like; but you put him in front of a movie camera, he's as wooden as a crucifix.

"What happened to your chest?" I asked him that day. It was gleaming, like a well-oiled baby's bottom. Take it from me, ours is not the sort of gym where people gleam.

"They shaved it, didn't they?" Yacoub sounded distinctly unhappy. "For that last Sri Lankan Airlines show. It's all the rage in Bollywood, apparently."

"Is *that* what they told you?"

"And that's not all they shaved," he continued in an aggrieved tone.

"Don't feel you have to tell us," I said quickly.

But he did. Had to get it off his chest, I suppose.

❋   ❋   ❋

"Rain!" shouted the director, "I want rain!" The rain towers were set up and for a full ten seconds it rained steadily. On the small screen of the monitor the house looked ravishing in the downpour. Damned photogenic, this house.

"You will see," said Batty, "how we Indians do things. You will see the difference when this commercial comes out."

"I will see," I agreed. The ad was for insurance policies or hair oil or something. It never really mattered. They all had the same storylines.

"Us Indians have ridden into town," declared Batty, "to teach you local cowboys a thing or two about films."

"And we Sri Lankans," I replied, "simply adore our foreign experts. Any expert as long as he's foreign, that's what we say. We'd pay good money to learn desert survival from Eskimos."

"Eskimos? What Eskimos? We're Indians," said Batty proudly. "We have the greatest film industry in the world."

There was no answer to that of course.

"That is why," he continued, "you Sri Lankans invite us over whenever you have anything important to shoot."

"Like the IPKF?"

"What's that?"

"Nothing, just clearing my throat. I have this terrible cough that won't go away."

I met Sanju at Wardrobe, already kitted out and made up. There wasn't much kitting out, he was already in his loincloth, though what this had to do with insurance I couldn't tell you. I was playing the grandfather, grey at the temples, in his Barbara Sansoni sarong, playing ball with little kids in the evening of his life, the dirty beast. No prizes for guessing who wrote the script. ("You will see what a difference a good script makes.") There was not much make-up in my case either. I was already grey at the temples.

Then we sat on the floor and waited to be called. And waited. And waited. Those of you who think acting is all glam please take note: most of your life is spent waiting for those brief twenty seconds of a take. And if you're really lucky they'll do it six or seven times. Then it's another couple of hours till the next shot. And so it goes on.

The actress and principal actor – I'll call him Twinkie because he really is famous and I'll never hear the end of it if I use his real name – were doing a steamy love scene in the Red Room, at one end of the house. This is our main guest-room and some years back we painted it a sexy shade of bordello red. Directors love it, guests hate it. No guest lasts longer than three days, which is probably a good thing anyway. I couldn't tell you what a steamy love scene had to do with insurance but I knew better than to ask.

Sanju and I were starving. We could hear the clash of stainless steel and the talk of unintelligible tongues issuing from the back kitchens where the Indian cooks were setting up shop. (Oh yes, the Indians travelled with cooks.)

"Sri Lankan food?" said Batty. "Don't make me laugh." Then he began to laugh. Then he began to hum the well-known Bollywood hit, *What a difference va day makes.*"

Truly, my mind by now was a haze of thosai-filled daydreams. Sanju's stomach was rumbling like a goods train at the Balana Pass. We were interrupted in our boredom by the second AD.

Now the second assistant director on set is the man everyone loves to hate, being more or less the personal body servant of the director. This one had three phrases in his vocabulary: yes Batty-ji, of course Batt-ji, *wonderful* Batty-ji.

"I have an important request," he began. He never looked at you when he spoke. He looked up, as if he was getting messages from God himself, which in a way he was.

"Twinkie would like to borrow a pair of boxer shorts. Would either of you gentlemen like to oblige?" The second AD smiled munificently, it was such a great honour he was bestowing on us. "The thing is, Twinkie's on the fourth take of his love scene." The second AD coughed delicately. "I'm afraid he got a little carried away with himself on the third."

"Don't look at me," Sanju said defiantly. "He certainly can't have my jockstrap. I've been sitting on this cold stone floor the last two hours and as it is my assets are completely frozen."

"I suppose I can help," I said a little reluctantly. I took him upstairs to the bedroom, where the wife was sitting at the dressing table writing out lamprijs recipes or something. I showed him my meagre selection. Of course he chose my favourite pair, didn't he, the ones with the little pink elephants on them.

The wife looked scandalised. "But that's your favourite pair," she objected, "you know they're the only ones not prone to wardrobe malfunctions."

I took her aside then and explained matters. "Look here," I said, "they're Indians, see. I think they deserve my fullest support."

"Make sure you get them back," she said sternly.

I turned to the second AD. "Make sure I get them back," I said sternly.

Much later I caught Twinkie briefly, wandering around in my shorts between takes.

"About those shorts. . ." I began.

"They're great, aren't they? I just love the little pink elephants."

"Do you think I could have them back when you're finished?"

"I'll have them laundered at the hotel and sent straight over to you."

"You really don't have to go to all that trouble. If you just give them back to me before you go…"

"Who owns this house?" he asked, interrupting.

"I do."

"Man, great house! Just like Amitabh Bachchan's, only more beautiful."

I basked in the glow of this precious nugget of information. For two seconds.

"But his is in Bombay, of course."

"Of course."

When my scene was over I found a crowd gathered under the Murano chandelier in the drawing room. There were two men on a rickety scaffolding trying with difficulty to raise it a foot or two.

"It's getting in the way of the shot," Batty explained.

The chandelier was shivering and shaking. So was I. Also quivering and quaking.

"Don't worry," Batty said airily. "If so much as a single crystal breaks I'll go straight out and buy you a new one. I find there are dozens of these at Moolchand's."

Twinkie was next to me in the crowd.

"About my shorts," I began.

Twinkie raised his hand. "Say no more."

It was then I noticed his arms. Not a single hair on them: scraped clean, with the curiously waxy look of those great slabs of pork hanging in the open air stalls along Airport Road. I thought of Yacoub, and the indignities he had been made to suffer for the greater good of Sri Lankan Airlines.

"You know what I'd really like?" said Twinkie. "What I'd really like is a picture of you hanging in my bedroom."

"Oh?" I didn't know whether to pat him on the back, or make a run for it.

"To remind me of what I need to look like when I get to your age."

❋   ❋   ❋

In the cinema world there is a certain etiquette that is observed about meals: nobody, but nobody, eats till the director does; and if the director happens to be off his food that day or a vegan with wind, that's your problem not his.

By now the sounds of Sanju's stomach were positively life-threatening. We were waiting for those magic words, "It's a wrap," the cinematic equivalent of "Dinner is served."

It was way past midnight when they declared. There was a mad dash by the Sri Lankans to the Indian buffet at the back. At the same time the doorbell rang and there was a mad dash by the Indians to the front. There were five delivery boys there on motorbikes.

"Pizza!" cried Batty joyously. "Food of the Gods!"

I waded through quite a few vadai. Then I went in search of Twinkie. I found him seated on the veranda steps, his face stuck into an enormous moon-shaped pizza.

"About my shorts," I began.

He pulled his face out of the pizza for a moment to look at me.

"What are you, a pervert or something?"

I left him sadly and walked on. I knew when I was beaten. In my mind I said goodbye to the little pink elephants.

The reels of film were flown to Bombay in the early hours of that morning itself and the ad was on air barely twelve nights later, numbing audiences nationwide, propelling many an insomniac

Colombo Uncle to instant sleep. I thought the back
of my head with its incipient bald patch looked
particularly exciting. But Batty was correct in his
predictions. At the F.A.T. Awards the following
month (Foreign Advertising Tomatoes), the ad won
six medals, including Gold, I believe, for foreign crew
with the most annoying nicknames.

The Good Little Ceylonese Girl

I remember. I remember the oil lamps flickering like fireflies on every step of the cement spiral up to Rosie's flat. The smell of acetylene torches in the gold shops, heavy and sweet in the night air. I remember Italo, the love of my life. I remember.

I came here to Biarritz, this wild corner of Europe, to write it all down. Now, ten years on, I almost feel I can. Actually I came to Paris first, but Paris was wet and miserable and there was someone practising the French horn in the next room, so I took the night train down with this bunch of Aussies I'd got in with, who travel the world in search of waves. In case you didn't know, Biarritz is the surfing capital of Europe.

Every day I sit, my back warming against the sea wall, scribbling away; and when I get tired I take up my board – the crappy white one they all laugh at – and head into the sea in search of the next wave. And the next. And the one after that. It's all in the timing, you see: get it right, and you shoot to shore on the

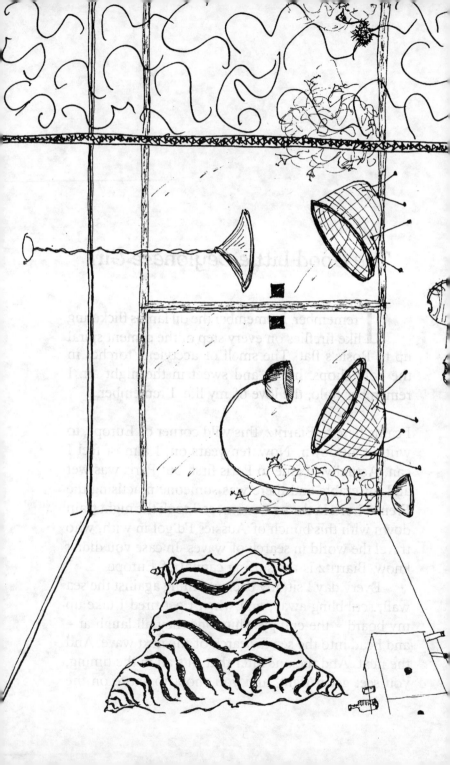

cusp of the wave – it's almost like flying! – and you land with a scrunch of sand at the feet of bemused onlookers and grannies sucking lollipops.

You may feel at times there are two people writing this. If you do, forgive me because there are. The twenty-one year old now scribbling away, and the eleven year old into whose heart she has finally managed to hack her way. So the sentiments are hers. The descriptions entirely mine.

ร ร ร

My father arrived in Somalia with five pounds sterling in his pocket. That was all you were allowed those days when you left Ceylon, as it was called back then in the Sixties. My brother and I tried bringing our goldfish along, in a Horlicks jar with holes drilled in the lid, but they were politely turned back at Customs and had to be handed over to Josie who came to see us off.

We were met by a welcoming party of the Ceylonese in Mogadiscio, all three of them: the Sinhalese Miss Madawela and the Tamil Sri Kanths. In addition there was Father Flavian, the only English speaking priest in those parts, who was there no doubt to safeguard our Catholic sensibilities.

Mrs. Sri Kanth was a jolly vegetarian in her forties with a fondness for sweet martinis, about the same age as my mother, the age that dared not show its leg. (My mother sometimes went as far as trousers but Mrs.

Sri was never to be seen out of sari.) Young Rosie
Madawela on the other hand wore short skirts and
chain smoked with attitude through a black plastic
holder, and sat on other people's divans with her legs
tucked up underneath. Her legs were smashing.

"Come here, little girl," she said patting the seat
next to her. "Come and sit down. Tell me your name."

"Suneeta."

"And how old are you?"

"Eleven."

"Come, sit. Don't be afraid."

I was torn. I felt instinctively that my mother
disliked Rosie Madawela. I could almost see the
conflicting emotions chasing each other through her
head. She didn't want me sitting next to Rosie.

But she must have also known I was that good
little Ceylonese girl, trained to obey, *trained by her*. I
went over and sat.

"You and I will be great friends, won't we?"

I nodded.

And that, you see, is how it all began.

After lunch that day they took us to the house assigned
my father by the UN, in Kilometre Four, one of a pair
of twin bungalows, turquoise and salmon pink, with
crazy x-shaped columns and octagonal porches. Rosie
led us through the house with the flourish of a
professional estate agent.

"And this will be your room, little girl," she said
raising the wooden window blinds with a great clatter.
Through the faded green of the mosquito netting I

saw the garden, fading yellow in the afternoon sunlight. My brother and I ran out to play and Rosie followed. She showed us its twisted casuarinas, its stunted bushes of wild tomato, the carpet of thorns where the lawn should have been. Paradise!

Then she stopped in front of a tree with light feathery leaves and yellow bell-shaped flowers, laden with soft green, geodesic pods.

"The kaneru tree," she said. "Incredibly poisonous." She broke off a pod. "Whatever you do, don't put one of these into your mouth."

"The tree of good and evil," I said solemnly and Rosie hooted with laughter.

༺ ༺ ༺

We live in someone's garage in the Rue de l'Université Americaine, just behind the gilded dome of Biarritz's Russian Orthodox church. There are a lot of us crammed into this tiny space, but it has this one great advantage: it is virtually free. The main house is being done up for an absentee Russian millionaire by his gang of workers. Paid next to nothing they are grateful for whatever we give them occasionally. I share my blanket with Russ who is large and uncomplicated. He laughs a lot and his timing is good. He doesn't think, which is even better.

This town was made famous a hundred and fifty years back by the wife of Napoleon III, the Empress Eugénie, who came here for its bracing sea air. I like

to imagine the plump little empress padding down to
sea every morning in her quilted bedroom slippers,
like I do, but this is only a figment of my fervid
imagination. In those days they only came to the
seaside in winter, and no doubt she was wheeled into
the waves in some extravagant wooden bathing
machine, shielded from the hungry gaze of the public
eye.

᷽   ᷽   ᷽

My brother and I were enrolled in the American
School in Mogadiscio. That first term he had a lot of
catching up to do and my mother sat with him every
afternoon. Rosie finished work at one, so when she
offered to take me off my mother's hands for the
afternoons my mother readily agreed.

"Look at the state of your feet!" she exclaimed
that first day she came to pick me up. "They're filthy!"

I told her how at break I had climbed over the
parapet wall that separated the school from the
scrubland of the wide open Somali plain, stretching
as far as the eye could see, in colours of smoky topaz
and goma green and burnt gold.

"You know you're not supposed to go out there!
What if you got eaten by a lion?"

This was, of course, going too far. Somalia those
days was full of lions. None as far as I knew attended
the American school. Rosie looked askance at my
pinafore, my long black pigtails, my Bata slippers: the

virtual uniform those days of every good little Ceylonese girl.

"What you need are some good closed shoes. I know just the place!"

We drove off in her Cinquecento, through Kilometre Four where I lived, and on past the spreading shanty town in the valley below. I remember the corrugated tin roofs of the shacks winking in the sun, as if people in them were sending out SOS signals. (And if they were nobody heard, certainly not the UN.) We drove into Old Town and round past the redbrick Parliament building, coming to a stop by Frutta Bertani, my mother's fruit and veg. shop.

"Come on, come on." Rosie leapt up three steps into a small shoe shop next door. We were greeted by the proprietor, an elderly lady in black dress, black cardigan, black shoes. But it was her blink that caught my eye, so to speak. I stood transfixed by those pouchy, slightly runny eyes that blinked several times a second: it seemed to me if egg-hoppers could blink this is what they would look like.

"Signora Tommiasi, Suneeta." I held out my hand in a sort of daze. I couldn't take in anything but the blink. How long had she had it? Had she been a blinking baby? Was it infectious? I vaguely registered that they were discussing a pair of camelskin shoes for me.

"Ciro!" Mrs. Tommiasi called out. "Ciro!"

A young Somali appeared from the back, tall, long limbs, no hips. He had a finely-chiselled skull-like head, tilted back.

He drew the shape of my foot on a piece of paper.
Rosie selected the colour of the skin, the shape of the
shoe: I used those shoes every day of my life till they
wore out on me, long after Rosie and I had parted
company.

The Somali held my foot in his curiously plump
fingers.

"This, little girl, is practically a perfect foot," he
said in a raspingly high, nails-across-the-blackboard
voice. Even now as I write this his voice is in my head,
scraping away at the insides, *the sitting tenant that refuses
to leave*.

But that day I hardly noticed. I was trying to figure
out ways of dragging my brother into the shop, to
introduce him to La Tommiasi, get him infected. A
little slave permanently on the blink would be no bad
thing for an older sister to own.

"Ci vediamo sta sera," whispered Ciro as we left.

"Maybe," said Rosie lightly. "Then again, maybe
not."

❧   ❧   ❧

There's a woman walking up and down the sand here.
She's been past twice now, looking hard each time.
I've seen her around – in Biarritz you soon get to know
the regulars. She's usually with an old boy nattily
dressed in white with a lemon pullover knotted round
his neck. At first I thought he was her father, an
unusually loving one. But Biarritz is full of couples
like this, and they can't all be fathers and daughters,

can they? She's what I would call a professional dolly-bird, always beautifully got up, false eyelashes, the lot. She must want to talk to me badly enough to get the toes of her Christian Louboutins badly scuffed in the sand.

Finally she stops and asks my name. Hers is Ella and she's here with her friend Uwe. Uwe who does crazy things. At the moment he's searching the world for the perfect sunset. She laughs, but the laugh sounds to me a little uncertain. She seems to feel I've fallen rather far below my station, me and my bodyboard. But I too can have a good life if I want to. All it takes is a little *presentation*, she says. Well you know what? I'm quite happy with Russ, thank you very much.

ॐ   ॐ   ॐ

Looking back, the thing I remember about Somalia was how gloriously politically incorrect it all was back then. People hung zebra skins on their walls. They wore elephant hair bracelets for luck and shark's teeth necklaces; and lion's claw earrings set in African gold, pure as it comes, clear yellow and soft like butter. There were enormous ostrich eggs, speckled and shiny, on people's coffee-tables, and silky dik-dik skins by their beds. The dik-dik was the marvellous spotted miniature deer of Somalia: people hunted and shot this creature so mercilessly I wouldn't be surprised if now, there isn't a single dik-dik left in all of East Africa.

I realise though how far ahead of her time Rosie was. She lived in a small flat up a cement spiral stairway, and the first thing that struck you when you entered was how spare and clean it all looked: green and white marble chip terrazzo floor, bare whitewashed walls devoid of ornament; devoid at least of anything that had snorted or bellowed or galloped in the recent past.

"Wherever possible I try not to take life, or be the cause of someone else taking it," she said, adding with a laugh, "Of course I'll kill anyone who suggests I do without my Italian leather shoes or handbags."

Rosie's father had been a vedah, a medicine man. She showed me an antique chest containing twenty or so miniature drawers, each labelled in the Sinhala script.

"My father's medicines. I brought the chest over after his death. A lot of it is very highly poisonous." She laughed. "So treat me nicely, or else."

"Do you have brothers and sisters?"

"One. A sister, back in Kalutara." She made a face. "You'll be meeting her quite soon. She's taking the banana boat out to spend Christmas with me." I could tell by the tone of her voice Rosie wasn't fond of her sister and wasn't particularly looking forward to her arrival.

"I only hope she'll meet some good-looking Italian on board who'll sweep her off her feet." She laughed. "Her one aim in life is to get married. It's a funny thing, it's those deserving cases that always get left behind. I think she tries too hard."

But good little Ceylonese girl that I was, it was Rosie I looked at with wonder: single, in her thirties, out on a limb in this wild corner of Africa, in a dead-end kind of job. And the amazing thing: she was supremely happy. I think she possessed some sort of secret that has eluded many of us all our lives.

Rosie's flat had a large terrace, bare but for a single meerschaum stove, a Somali cooking pot into which you put live coals before grilling your meat on top. I don't think it had ever been used. But the balcony held one major attraction: it overlooked an open air cinema next door playing a constantly running film, usually a Hindi movie. It never mattered where you left off, you could always catch it another day, or even a couple of hours later: they just kept running the reels over and over. In time I became quite proficient in all those jerky, hip-wriggling, round-the-coconut-tree routines.

ھ   ھ   ھ

I look at Russ and the boys curling around the inside of these giant waves, flipping and somersaulting happily on their boards, and I am reminded of those brave foolish birds who fly straight into the open jaws of the African crocodile, to peck away between its yellowing teeth. Me, I just lie on the back of the great green beast, listening to the beat of its heart pounding away, way below the range of the human ear. But I can hear, I can feel.

ও ও ও

"We're going somewhere different today. I'm going to introduce you to my special friend. I don't think you've met him."

Rosie turned the car down a lane in Kilometre Four, somewhere close to where I lived.

Several turns later we came to a stop at a dead-end. There were various shrubs and thorn bushes so you hardly saw the door set low in the wall, the colour of verdigris. If you didn't know, you couldn't even imagine there was a house behind, it was so well hidden. Taking a key from her bag Rosie unlocked the door. We passed through a small walled garden, fronting a low one-storey house with glass doors and iron grill-work.

The doors slid open. Rosie was wrong. I had met him before: the young Somali from the shoe shop. I was once again struck by how long and lean he looked next to Rosie's diminutive figure as she stood on tiptoe to kiss him.

"Ciao Ciro," she said.

"Ciao bella!" He turned to me. "Your shoes are ready," he said.

But I had seen something move in the small courtyard beyond. I walked through the living room with its bucket chairs in woven black and white plastic cane, the zebra skin rug, the wooden camel bells, and out through the sliding doors at the back.

A small purple baby ostrich stood there, no more than two feet high, craning its dusty neck to reach the shoe flowers on the bushes.

"I see," said the shrill-guttural voice behind me, "you've met the love of my life. His name is Italo. You can pet him if you like."

We stayed the whole afternoon, Ciro putting on Beatles records and Rosie knocking up a hasty puttanesca most of which Ciro devoured before they dropped me home early evening. I have an enduring vision of the two of them doing the twist on the back terrace, to the sounds of "I Wanna Hold Your Hand" – Ciro hunched over Rosie's upturned smiling face like some sort of demented dentist – while Italo and I stood around watching open-mouthed, as if it was our turn next.

By some unspoken arrangement with Rosie I omitted any mention of Ciro to my parents. They disapproved of Rosie anyway and the fact of her having a boyfriend might have meant my not being allowed to see her at all. What I came to realise, though, is that in those magical months before Christmas Rosie came to represent for me all that was real: I lived, ate and breathed for those afternoons with her, and my home life became the unreal part, the negative of the true picture.

This is not to say my parents didn't exist. Of course they did, they were ever-present, the Gods illuminated on the temple walls, lamplit and flickering. But you stopped a moment to look around, you found there was very little there, only ikons, whose meaning had somehow got lost in translation. Real life had escaped outside, into the sunlight under the trees, with its flexing muscles, its beating heart.

ᘡ   ᘡ   ᘡ

I have arranged to meet Ella at her hotel for drinks.
She's staying – where else? – at Biarritz's Hôtel du
Palais, the palace built for the empress right there on
the beach. The doorman looks at my grubby feet but
lets me in because Ella has had the good sense to come
to the front to meet me. Inside everything is gilded to
within an inch of its life and there's a mink trapped
inside a glass cage, and lots of blackened boulle
furniture. She takes me into the white and gold dining
room where you can watch the crescent shaped bay
and the crashing waves outside through the safety of
the glass.

"Isn't it magnificent?" she murmurs, but I shiver,
because I know this is the time the sea gets ravenous,
and with a sudden snap of its jaws it can crunch you
up if you're foolish enough to be in the water at this
hour.

ᘡ   ᘡ   ᘡ

I remember the perfect crescent of beach bordered by
liquid crystal sea where my father took us every Sunday
morning to give my mother her lie-in. But in the
afternoon there was Sunday school, in the dusty
sacristy of Mogadiscio cathedral.

There were eight of us in the class, Episcopalians
from Boston, Syriac Christians from Kerala,
Maronites from Beirut and plain old Catholics like
us.

"Evil," said Father Flavian wiping the beads of sweat from his thinning scalp, "will always be present in your life. Remember that. As long as you have free will, you have the freedom to choose: between good and bad, right and wrong."

"What about animals, Father? What about children?"

Father Flavian looked at me a little grimly. You were lucky to catch him sober after six. It was now four-thirty and you could tell the strain on him was rather great. "Animals don't have free will, my child, so obviously they can't commit evil. Children are another matter. The important thing," he continued, "is to bear in mind that you can never achieve good through evil means. The goodness of the result is always obliterated by the badness of the action."

"But what about war, Father? Isn't it OK to kill if you think by doing so you're going to prevent further deaths?"

"The normal rules don't apply during war," he said sharply. I think what he meant was, Suneeta don't be difficult.

I began whispering to my brother.

"Perhaps Suneeta would like to tell us what she finds so interesting," said Father Flavian wearily.

"I always thought, Father, it wasn't the apple on the tree in the Garden of Eden that got us into all this trouble. It was the pair on the ground."

"Ha, bloody, ha."

"What's that, Father?"

"Nothing, my child. Nothing."

My parents picked us up after class. Siesta-time was over and shops had opened their doors, all lit up and decorated because Christmas was a big event in Mogadiscio. It was still only a few years after independence and the Italian presence was very strong on the streets. My father parked the car just by the Zanussi store, and we all got out. Turning into a side street we walked into what might have been medieval Cairo: twisted mud alleys with open drains running down the middle, many-storeyed whitewashed houses with deep-set turquoise windows. Further in was Mr. Hassan's gold shop. Gold was cheap and widely available, and people said Somali gold was the purest in the world. Most goldsmiths including Mr. Hassan were Indian. They sat in their little shops under green Naptha flares, the sweetish all-pervasive smell of their acetylene torches heavy in the night air.

I remember him showing my mother a particularly beautiful piece of work that day, a pair of earrings fashioned like birdcages: inside the cage instead of birds there were loose jewels, pink and green and blue, and as you moved the stones rattled.

"Not for sale, I'm afraid," said Mr. Hassan.

That was the wrong thing to say to my mother. "And why not?" she demanded.

"They're a client's private design. Done to order."

"Actually they're for me," said a high voice behind us. I knew the voice, I didn't have to turn around. When I did, he looked straight through me as if I didn't exist. He was with a very good-looking Somali girl.

"I'll have them wrapped up for you," said Mr. Hassan. They left the shop while we were still browsing and at the door he gave me this weird stare. I thought, am I being warned?

"A very good client," said Mr. Hassan. "Always ordering things." His eyes twinkled. "Many girlfriends."

Next day I told Rosie.

"Describe the earrings," she ordered. I told her about the beautiful birdcages. Rosie laughed. She didn't normally do bitter; this time she came quite close.

"Were they anything like these?" She held up the identical pair.

It was not up to me to ask why she was hanging around with a guy who was so obviously unfaithful. I was just learning my way around this complicated adult world: I didn't understand it much then: I still don't.

೯ ೯ ೯

Ella's friend Uwe joins us on the terrace as the sun begins to set.

"How about a little champagne, ma chérie?"

Uwe has skinny legs and tiny feet encased in pointy leather loafers, and there is an air of preciousness about him. While they are discussing the relative merits of Dom Perignon and vintage Laurent Perrier I sit there bored, between the salted macadamias and the stuffed olives.

I begin a mild flirtation with the hovering waiter who is Vietnamese or something. I feel a certain affinity with him at any rate because he's from somewhere east of the Suez. Reminds me of that old joke they used to tell back then when you were allowed to tell these things: What's the difference between a Ceylonese and a Vietnamese? Half an hour in the oven, of course.

৯ ৯ ৯

Exams were coming up and I had to work hard because I was under probation those first three months. If I did badly it would mean having to go down a class.

About this time I remember the *panettones* made their first appearance in Mogadiscio. They arrived that festive season like a flock of gold and silver coloured birds, and everyone gave everyone else one. I have eaten many panettones since, and they were nothing like as bad as ones you got back then: dry and papery, hard to chew, impossible to swallow. Once you put a piece in your mouth all human conversation ceased. It was a surprisingly useful way of silencing your more talkative guests. Somebody presented us with a particularly vile one in its truncated pyramid shaped box, cobalt blue with little silver stars all over. My brother and I used it for football practice. It got slightly dented in one corner and my mother was furious. I remember her presenting it to Mrs. Sri Kanth as a sort of jolly, vegetarian, pre-Christmas offering.

Then Rosie came to school waving a thin blue aerogramme in my face. "She's coming next Saturday, my sister!"

She got permission from my parents to take me off to Merca, ninety kilometres south, where the boat docked. It was expected late afternoon so we left late, stopping off for a goat sandwich on the Afgoi road just before the Merca turn-off. The sandwich was quite old, the goat inside even older, and I threw away most of it. Further on Rosie stopped to take a picture of a particularly beautiful one-humped white Somali camel, but got shooed away by the irate owner who waved his stick at us. Whether he didn't want us to steal his soul or whether he disapproved of women photographers I couldn't tell.

At Merca we parked the car and walked to the almost deserted customs warehouse. There was no quayside and passengers were lifted to shore in a sort of basket. It was quite a tricky operation. Only last month Mrs. Barber at the American Embassy had lost her grand piano which tipped into the Indian Ocean with a mighty crash.

The ship was a speck on the horizon. It didn't seem to be moving at all and I couldn't believe it would get to us that afternoon. We tramped around those streets, their severe Mussolini facades deserted and darkening at sunset, and I had an ominous sense of foreboding, of something bad about to happen, like in a de Chirico painting.

It was almost dark when the basket landed on shore. The customs and immigration formalities were over very quickly and a tall figure came towards us, taking off her straw hat, shaking loose her curly long hair. She was elegant in a way Rosie was not, with a beautiful, slightly enigmatic look on her face.

"Meet my sister Devika," said Rosie in a small voice.

We piled into the bug Fiat and headed home. I don't think Devika spoke ten words the entire trip. Rosie gabbled on, a running commentary, and Devika just sat there looking round, looking cool.

The thing about Devika was – and I only realize this now – Devika didn't say much because actually she didn't have much to say. They say still waters run deep. In this case they hardly ran at all. But she had the looks to match the beautiful silences: the classic Sinhala *konde krail*, the slightly prominent jaw, the long eyes tipped up at the corners, resigned in their infinite wisdom.

You could imagine her running through paddy fields in her colourful batik cloth with other village girls. And how wrong you would be!

Whether by accident or design, I hardly saw Devika once she was established back at Rosie's.

"Where is she?" I asked every afternoon.

"Oh, gone out somewhere. Sleeps late you know, never gets up before noon. This is like morning to her. My old father used to say she turns night into day and day into night."

"Like a vampire, you mean?"

"Oh, shut up!"

But I got information from other sources. At home my father said to my mother: "You know that good-looking sister of Rosie's? She's all over town with that odd Somali chap. Lots of gossip at the office."

Then one Sunday morning I saw her at the beach!

"Look, there's Rosie," said my brother.

"Don't be silly, that woman's much taller. And she's got long hair."

It wasn't Rosie at all. It was Devika, in a bikini the colour of double cream that deliciously set off her café-au-lait complexion. The real surprise was that she was up and about so early. I noticed the figure behind her. Ciro.

How I longed to tell Rosie! But I knew it would cause her immense sadness and I could bear anything but that. The good little Ceylonese girl was beginning to learn her lessons well.

ക്ക ക്ക ക്ക

The champagne arrives. One of each, because they haven't been able to decide which to order. And I don't even like the stuff. Ella and Uwe are staring at me with pained, disappointed expressions on their faces like parents whose child has unaccountably failed them in some way.

"What?"

"Mais voyons, chérie, qu'est que tu cherches?" Ella repeats crossly.

I don't answer. It would take too long to explain anyway. Instead I look out towards the beach where the lights are coming on one by one and the last of the stragglers make their way home.

৯৯ ৯৯ ৯৯

"Welcome!" said Mrs. Sri swaying slightly. "So good of you to come, so good." It was the day of her much anticipated welcome party for Devika, the usual UN crush, the usual UN food. Somalia was considered a hardship station, with a duty-free commissary operating every Thursday afternoon where you could buy Rémy Martin in frosted green bottles for one dollar seventy-two, and stuffed oysters flown in from the West coast of America, and sevruga in little round yellow tins. Life was very hard indeed.

There was lots of smoke and wine, and French, Italian, Somali and English all spoken at high speed like a simultaneous translation gone badly wrong. There was the usual sprinkling of Ministers observing their self-imposed no-alcohol rule, absorbing whiskey through large and opaque tumblers of coke.

Someone had brought a record player out onto the terrace and they were playing Astrid Gilberto. I don't know quite how Ciro got in – I am sure Mrs. Sri would not have invited him. Almost as soon as I spotted him the music changed, the mellow Brazilian bossa nova replaced by that edgy, slightly frenzied music the Sixties were so famous for: and suddenly, predictably, Ciro was dancing with Devika, holding one of her hands in his. This time, I noticed, he didn't have to hunch so much.

Next day Devika joined us for lunch all tousled up, in a long white towelling robe, devastatingly attractive, picking at her pasta in a dreamy sort of way.

"So who's the little ice-breaker then?" Rosie asked, rather icily.

Devika shook her head slowly, running fingers through her luxuriant hair. She moved sparingly, with great economy of movement, her every gesture invested with a sort of measured significance as if it were the most important thing on earth. I think this was part of her great attraction: when she looked at you she held your gaze steadily, you couldn't look away. You felt you were the only thing that mattered to her in this big bad world.

"That lovely Mrs. Sri Kanth. . . " she said. "Present for me. . .over there." She closed her eyes as if the effort of speech had been too much. Rosie and I looked at the box, cobalt blue and silver, with the slight dent in the corner. I opened the flap. The cake still nestled inside in its cellophane packing, a long rip across the top where my brother had once tried to open it.

"I think we should give it to Ciro," suggested Rosie brightly. "He'll eat anything, a real dustbin."

"By the way," said Devika slowly, looking down at the table as if she was reading from a script, "I think he wants to speak to you."

"He does, does he? He can tell me himself then. Doesn't have to send messages through other people."

Since Devika's arrival we had been going a lot to Ciro's but he was hardly ever there. Rosie would let herself in with her key, put a record on and hurl herself into one of those bucket chairs, tucking her legs up. I would make a beeline out the back to play with Italo the ostrich. He loved shoe flowers and I loved holding him up so he could reach the ones at the top.

We also took to driving around Mogadiscio in the dead hours of the afternoon when shops were closed and people were at their siesta. Sometimes we ended up at the Bar Fiorella for a drink before Rosie dropped me home. I always had a Mau-Mau, the bitter orange bottled drink; Rosie had one too with Campari and ice in hers. I remember Mogadiscio as a beautiful town then, all public squares and fountains and triumphal arches: Fascist architecture that almost persuaded you it had once been part of a great empire. The town even had pavements unlike the Colombo we had so recently left.

Always on these trips Rosie came to a stop outside the Murano chandelier shop next to the Banca Nazionale del Lavoro. It hadn't yet opened for the evening but we were content to sit in the car watching the rays of late afternoon sunlight cut through coloured droplets of glass, turquoise and amber and amethyst.

"One day," Rosie sighed, "one day there'll be one of these in every room in the house. I've promised myself that."

"What, here in the flat?" I asked, a little confused.

"No, silly, back home."

I began to get worried, "Rosie, are you going back? You can't leave me, I've only just met you!"

"No dear, I don't want to." She paused a moment. A single tear rolled down her face.

"Rosie, what's wrong?"

She shook her head, wiping the tear away with the back of her hand. The sun had almost gone in. One by one the chandeliers receded into darkness where they continued to glow, softly, like coals after the fire has died down.

"He's bleeding me," she said finally. "I don't think I can take much more."

"What do you mean bleeding you?"

She looked at me as if I was stupid or something.

"Money, darling, money. He gets me to pay for everything. You know those earrings? They were supposed to be a present from him. Who do you think paid for them?"

I looked at her in silence.

"Have you ever wondered how a man who works in a shoe shop can afford to live in Kilometre Four?"

She started the car up. "And now my sister," she said.

৯ ৯ ৯

The boys are thinking of moving on. The sea gets colder towards Christmas and Biarritz can be pretty miserable in the rain. They're talking of Arugam Bay on the east coast of Sri Lanka where the waves are legendary. Russ says he'll definitely go whatever I decide. There's another boy here, Marco, who's had his eye on me quite a while now, and I know he wants to stay on. The choice is mine, stay or go. I wonder, am I in danger of turning into some sort of low-rent dolly-bird myself?

Do I really care?

❦   ❦   ❦

Exams began. First day was Maths and I didn't do too well. Today, if I could turn the clocks back to the start of that day, I would. If I could be the director of the movie and say, *cut, let's do that bit again*, I would. But unlike in cinema, you get one take and one take only. Life's a black comedy and all performances are live.

"Let's go to Ciro's," Rosie said when she picked me up, "I need to sort out some stuff with him when he gets home."

We let ourselves in and I went straight out the back to Italo. The stupid bird turned his head away from me. I hadn't seen him for a while and he was going to make me suffer. So I ignored him for a bit. Then I couldn't stand it anymore. I grabbed him and stuck my nose in that soft underbelly, dusty and flea-ridden. Italo squawked with pleasure.

I could hear Rosie rummaging about in the kitchen.

"He's out of oil, he's out of tomato paste," she called out. "Don't move, I'll be back in a minute."

The Cinquecento roared off down the road.

Then I heard the sound of water running. It was odd hearing that, in the parched stillness of the African afternoon. I started chasing Italo round and round the yard. It was one of our best games. With a silent *whoosh!* the doors slid open.

I stopped in my tracks, the blood pounding in my head. He was standing there. In that long white robe Devika had worn. He didn't say anything. Just stood there, watching.

"What are you doing?" I stammered.

"Not well," he whispered hoarsely. "Didn't go to work." He looked like a monk in a medieval picture, gaunt and attenuated.

"Vieni," he whispered, "vieni qui."

I stood there frozen in fear: the dik-dik caught in the headlamps on the wide African plain. He sank into a bucket chair, patting his lap, beckoning me with strange animal noises.

"Vieni," he whispered again, urgently.

But you see, he needn't have worried: I was that good little Ceylonese girl, trained to obey, too frightened to run: it was beyond my capability to do anything else. I began to walk towards him, the clockwork doll wound up and set on its preordained path. I climbed onto his lap.

He made strange crooning noises, stroking my hair.

There was a sudden crash at the door. Rosie had dropped the bottle of oil.

"Ciro!" she screamed, running towards him. "Bastard!"

I scrambled off Ciro's lap but he sat there unmoved. And the funny thing, I was the one who felt ashamed, I was the one who felt guilty.

"How could you!" Rosie was sobbing. "Suneeta, go outside!"

I went out into the backyard, sliding the door shut. I could hear her through the glass screaming at him. My legs were shaking. It was difficult to breathe. I picked up Italo and cuddled him, burying my face in that warm body. At that moment he was the only thing I had, the only thing that mattered.

"How could you," Rosie kept repeating, "*how could you!*" But Ciro just sat there, like a child whose ice cream has been taken away.

"Anything I want," I heard him say, "anyone I want."

I raised Italo high as he would go to reach the shoe flowers at the top, and he was gobbling away like a machine. Suddenly, without warning my legs gave way, and at the same time I wet myself. We collapsed together in a heap, a warm feral bundle of feathers and urine.

I don't know how I got through the rest of that week, exams every day. But children are tougher than adults, girls toughest of all. Maybe when you're young you don't know the vocabulary of evil so it's almost as if the evil doesn't exist. Then you grow up, you learn the words: a far more frightening proposition.

"I'll never let him get anywhere near you again," Rosie promised tearfully.

She was wrong.

Two days later I was on her balcony as usual, practising a Hindi dance routine, all piyaar this and piyaar that, when a thin strip of shadow fell diagonally across the cement. I looked up to find him watching me.

I instinctively moved to put the stove between us. I was ready for him this time. I had prepared my weapon of mass distraction. "There's a blue box on the table," I said, "with silver stars. It's a cake. I know Rosie wanted you to have it."

When he heard the word 'cake' he went inside, and a little while later I heard the click of the front door.

But when I went inside myself I found the cake still on the table.

ॐ   ॐ   ॐ

There's Marco and me now, and two others, and it's quite lonely. I wonder if I did the right thing; but I must finish this story before anything else. Ella comes to the beach to say goodbye. The sunsets really have been not very good and they're off to Quinto do Lago in Portugal to try their luck there. "Uwe's really disappointed when he doesn't get what he wants." She looks at me sideways. "What will you do?"

What will I do? Maybe I'll sneak into the hotel and release the mink from its glass cage, maybe that's what I'll do. *Free a fur today and liberate yourself!*

And then?

Then there's always the next wave, and the next, and the one after that: to sweep me out beyond the rocks and past the headland, out into open water. But even the waves conspire against me. All they ever do is shoot me straight back to shore each time.

ও ও ও

"Come on," said Rosie, "I'm taking you out for a celebration drink." Exams were over. I had come second. We drove to the Bar Fiorella. It was quite noisy inside; there were three old boys huddled over the radio listening to a football match in Italy. We sat at the zinc-top bar on high stools and had our usual – Mau-Mau on the rocks for me, Mau-Mau with Campari for her.

"There's something I have to tell you," she said over the noise. "I'm leaving."

"What!" I could hardly keep the shock out of my voice.

"I broke up with Ciro. Gave him his marching orders."

"I don't believe it!"

"After what he tried to do to you…You honestly think I'd stick on?"

"What did he say?"

"He threatened me." She gave a little laugh. "It's all right, I'm a big girl, I can handle it. His rent's paid up three more months, and by then I'll be long gone, on the boat back with Devika." The corners of her mouth twitched. "Anyway I gave him a wonderful leaving present. His gratuity. I gave him the cake."

I was silent for a long while.

"What will you do back in Ceylon?"

"What I always do, I guess. Land on my feet."

"So I won't be seeing Italo again," I said sadly.

"Are you crazy?" Rosie was almost savage, "You want to go back there for seconds?" Then she thought for a bit. "I have to extract my key from him, though. But you wait in the car."

Of course I followed her in.

"Ciro!" she called out. She never usually announced our arrival. Maybe now they were no longer together she felt it necessary. "Ciro!"

There was silence.

We slid open the doors and went in. It was quite dark inside and the air was heavy with a slightly fetid smell, as if an animal had been caged inside for a long time.

Then we saw him sitting in the gloom, motionless, in his white towelling robe. Rosie drew in her breath sharply and bent over him. There was a thin line of vomit at the corner of his mouth. He was cold.

Rosie was half sobbing, half screaming, "Oh my God, oh my God!" Then she did an odd thing. She began sniffing all around him. The cake was on the table in front, out of its blue and silver box, the remains of a slice on a plate. She sniffed that and immediately straightened up.

"Bitch!" she screamed. "Bitch! How dare she come here and ruin things for all of us! We were fine as we were, we would have worked things out!" She started crying.

But I ignored her. I had other things on my mind. "Who'll feed Italo?" I asked. "He's trapped in the courtyard. You *know* ostriches can't fly."

"It's only a bloody bird," snapped Rosie. I pushed past and went out the back, leaving the doors wide open. I tried to drive Italo through to the front. The stupid bird thought I was playing games and ran round and round in circles. Then it dashed into the house with its weird gait, like a one-legged shopper in a hurry, screeching and flapping, knocking over chairs and camel bells. It landed with a squawk on the dead man's lap.

Bad move.

I grabbed him tightly and ran out front. Opening the little street door I hurled him out with all my might. He took off at a smart clip down the road, in a flurry of feathers, complaining. I stood there panting, watching him go, praying he would be all right.

Rosie put the cake back almost tenderly into its box, together with the half-eaten piece. She carefully rinsed the knife and plate and put them away. We drove away in the car with the cake sitting next to her on the front seat, and I was such a good little girl I didn't even ask for a piece. There was no sign of Italo on the road though I kept looking out for him all the way home. Rosie stopped the car outside our house.

"Not a word to anyone, understand?" I nodded.

"One thing you need to know," she said fiercely.

"Us adults. We're only ever doing the best we can. Remember that. We're not perfect. *We don't always get it right!*"

Can you be good and bad at the same time? Can a person achieve good results through evil means? These are not questions I have given much thought to either then or since, though in my place Father Flavian might have had the answer. All I know is that Rosie was my guardian angel, there for me when I needed her. And wasn't I the lucky one!

But what of the other, good little Ceylonese girls? Because as you know, there were many of us back then, a whole generation almost. What of them?

Well let me tell you, not a week, not a *day* goes by that I don't think of them, and wonder about their well-being, and hope they too pulled through all right. Because I fear, just as much as you do, not many were quite so lucky.

I remember Rosie driving off that day in a cloud of dust, the radio blaring I Wanna Hold Your Hand. I watched her go, sad, because I was losing my first real friend, the first to give me even an inkling that adults don't always play by the straight, the obvious rules.

Then I dug deep into my pinafore pocket and fished out the last two remaining kaneru seeds, soft green, geodesic, the ones I hadn't used. I threw them in the bushes and went inside. I remember.

The Maharajah of Patragarh

The Maharajah of Patragarh was dreaming again. He sat on the roof of his sandstone castle taking in the early morning sun on a splendid reclining chair. The chair was curved in an elongated S-shape, rather like a magic carpet about to unfurl in preparation for flight. And in a sense this is exactly what it was, for when the Maharajah sat there, it allowed his mind to roam far and free over the eight long centuries of his family's existence.

And what an existence! How many invasions there had been in that time! The Moghul Emperors of Old Delhi, the English Viceroys of New: Patragarh had turned its back firmly on all of them. His richer, grander cousins – rulers of neighbouring states – had cosied and cuddled for all they were worth, the taste of Cherry Blossom on their lips, reaping honours and rewards far beyond their wildest dreams. How they had squabbled among themselves over the order of their precedence, the size of their gun salutes! A classroom of overgrown schoolboys before their imperial schoolmaster.

The Maharajah of Patragarh had asked for nothing. And that is precisely what he had got.

While he slept the Maharajah's mind flew free as a bird over the remaining extent of his property. It wasn't a large castle, an acre at most, surrounded by a moat. But it was built in the purest Hindu style with splendid Bo-leaf battlements, and pinnacled domes inside each turret. There was no flirtation here with the prevailing Islamic Moghul fashion, the white marble with its inlaid pietra dura that had so easily seduced his cousins. None of the tawdry tinsel, the gaudy mirrorwork that adorned their bigger, flashier palaces. His small rooms were mostly painted, in the slightly sharp, high colours of the eighteenth century.

His cousins kept abreast of the times. (It was easy to do when you had the money.) They had air-conditioning. He had cross-ventilation. As far as *he* was concerned it was enough. His household froze in winter and baked in summer. But they had been freezing and baking for eight centuries. It was nothing new.

The Maharajah sighed in his sleep as his mind's eye saw the cracked sandstone slabs of his roof. The dome in one of the turrets had been demolished in his father's day to make way for a galvanized iron water tank. It gave the castle a curiously lop-sided air. How he longed to rebuild that dome!

But the moat was dry now. A single bedraggled peacock picked disconsolately at the weeds in its bed. It was all so difficult. If you were a Maharajah, by virtual definition you were fabulously wealthy. So how could you tell people you were down to your last castle? They would laugh.

The Maharajah of Patragarh stirred uneasily and opened his eyes, and as he did the chimes of a Meissen clock floated up from the courtyard below. Nine o'clock. He rose with difficulty to his feet. He was not as young as he used to be and every day it got more difficult. But then he remembered eight centuries of the bluest of blue Hindu blood coursing through his veins and his back straightened imperceptibly.

"*Show time*," he said.

The young Sri Lankan couple was in India on honeymoon. Five nights and six days in the Golden Triangle the agent had advertised. He had unaccountably failed to mention the average age of the tour which was about eighty-seven. Five nights and six days of detailed and non-stop discussions, on arthritis and bowel movements, hip replacements and incontinence. Even at the Taj Mahal, in the heart of the no-pollution zone, talk had very quickly descended to the sordid matter of Mrs. Marawila's loose motions. It had been a relief to pay extra and get away for the day.

The white Ambassador car bumped across the dry moat and came to a stop outside the immensely high doorway studded with iron nails.

"I wonder if some loony old Maharajah will come roaring out with a loaded shotgun?" the boy joked with the girl. But in the event the small doorway cut into the large one was opened by a dignified old retainer in a smart red coat and turban.

He bowed. "The tickets are twenty rupees each but you can pay at the end. Let me take you round first."

"The sort of cook-appu every decent house should have," the girl whispered.

They took in the small throne-room with its faux-gilt furniture, overlooked by the narrow gallery curtained in muslin where women of the house sat in purdah. They were shown the little Chinese desk from which the Maharajah had run his country of a few hundred square miles. There was a table for sixteen in the dining room, but the furniture was of that plain serviceable sort you find in up-country estate bungalows. Strangely, there were no photographs anywhere.

They ascended the narrow ramp to the roof.

It was the splendid chair that first attracted their attention.

"Oh look!" the girl said to the boy. Then they noticed the elderly figure in jam jar glasses snoring gently, his face turned towards the weak rays of the mid-morning sun.

"Is that ... surely it can't be the . . .?"

"Certainly not," said the old retainer rather quickly. "That's Nath, his faithful manservant. His Highness is away at one of his other palaces."

"Can I take a picture?"

The retainer put his finger to his lips. "Of course. But please don't wake him up. At this time of his life he really needs his sleep."

They looked out over the battlements at the town, a sea of small dust-coloured houses with flat roofs. A little boy on a neighbouring roof waved at them.

"Girl!" he shouted in thin, clear, piercing tones. "Girl! What your name? Where you from?"

"Where exactly are you from?" the retainer asked them.

"Sri Lanka," the boy replied.

"Oh, I remember... I remember His Highness telling us. When he was up at Cambridge as a young man he had a Sri Lankan friend. He went over there once for the holidays, to a house in Colombo. And he was so impressed with Sri Lankan hospitality he gifted them a Jaguar when he left."

The boy laughed. "And the jaguar gobbled up every living creature in the house, I suppose?"

But the old retainer was lost in thought for a moment. There was water in his rheumy eyes. "It was a Jaguar motor-car," he said softly.

Downstairs they paid the forty rupees for their two tickets. The old retainer wouldn't hear of a tip. But the young girl with her sharp Sri Lankan eyes had noticed the nondescript furniture. She had seen the enamel basins put out to catch the leaks in the sandstone roof.

"Please," she said. "I'd like to contribute something to the upkeep of this amazing building. I know it can't be easy."

"His Highness wouldn't hear of it," was the sharp reply.

The girl shrugged and turned to go.

"But if you really want to help, there's Nath up there. You noticed the glasses he was wearing. Cataract in both eyes. We're getting up a collection for the operation."

"Of course, my pleasure!" The girl handed over a thousand-rupee note.

The Ambassador bumped away over the rutted track carrying the young couple back to civilization, and the Problem of Incontinence in Sri Lanka Today. The retainer watched them go. Then he mounted the ramp to the roof. That was the worst about living in a castle. The heights. Every year the climbing got a little more difficult.

He reached the sleeping figure on the roof and stood over him for a moment, watching. But the sleeper woke with a start and in one fluent movement that belied his advanced years he sank to the ground.

"Maharaj-ji, Maharaj-ji," he mumbled kissing the other's feet and the edge of his red coat. "It's so good of you to let me sleep up here in your chair all day, in this the evening of my years."

The other touched the top of his head, the signal that he could rise in the royal presence. "Go down to the kitchens," he said gently. "Your lunch will be getting cold.

"Oh, and take off those ridiculous glasses. You'll go blind if you wear them too long."

The Jack Fruit

They threw the letter down to him in the pit he was digging. It was hot for September. The sun had dried the skin on his bare back to paper and he could almost hear it crackle as he wielded in turn the pickaxe and the spade. Through the cracks in his papery skin he could feel the pin-pricks of sweat.

Inside the pit the air was moist.

"London clay," Sonny said, "a bugger to dig."

"Keep the walls of the pit straight," Sonny said. There was a natural tendency to dig inwards so the base of the pit got smaller as you went down, and Ashoka had to make a special effort to keep the walls straight, the hole square.

The muscles on his back had turned to cords of woven steel and down at the gym he found he could curl forty kilos without a murmur: professional bodybuilders – and they had biceps the size of Ashoka's head – curled only thirty, bellowing while they did like bulls to slaughter. The blocks of water-logged soil weighed more than any iron; Ashoka had

learned the trick of levering them on to the edge of the spade, then over his shoulder and out of the pit.

He was three foot down and still no sign of the drain. It really didn't matter; even a lifetime of this digging would have left him unfazed. He was supremely fit, supremely happy. This was, he thought, his perfect half-hour.

He told his best mate on site Jason about the Sri Lankan jack fruit. How it took months and months to grow, reaching sometimes the size of a small child. But it attained perfection for just half an hour of its very long life. He had seen one at Harrods Food Hall once. It lay dead on a bed of marble, surrounded by crushed ice under a spotlight. Price, eighty pounds, and way beyond its perfect half-hour.

Jason laughed. "This may be your perfect half-hour, mate. Mine's still a long way off."

The letter was in a brown OHMS envelope from the Home Office, perfectly courteous and polite. It gave him twenty-eight days to leave the country.

"Throw it away," Jason advised. "Vanish. That's what everyone else does. Sonny can move you from site to site. They'll never find you." It was easy for Jason to say. He was born in England. Nobody could throw him out: he could afford the luxury of his low-minded principles.

Ashoka took half-day off and went to the Immigrants Advisory Service in the Strand, up a grey carpeted stairway above a chemist. There were two sleek Asian girls in there, typing away like express trains. They ignored him. He sat down on an orange foam sofa of indeterminate shape and began reading the monochrome leaflets put out carefully on display. Like all things free they were boring as hell.

"Yes?"

Ashoka looked up. The better looking of the two girls was regarding him coolly through her horizontal black-framed specs. He hurriedly got to his feet and handed her the letter. She looked at his sweat-stained tee shirt and the black London clay under his finger nails. Just because I'm free, her glance seemed to say, don't think you can take liberties.

She read the letter through without comment. Ashoka remained on his feet. He noticed her black hair that fell in a single movement from one side of her neck to the other, like a piece of thick, expensive cloth. Hot, Ashoka thought. Lots of attitude.

She looked up. "Go home," she said. "Write a letter to your local MP appealing against this decision."

"Who is my MP? Where do I find him?"

She looked at him without mercy.

"That's for you to find out.

"And don't even *think* of going dressed like that."

* * *

Ashoka lived at his place of work. The site was one of six houses on St. Alphonsus Road all owned by the same syndicate. By day he was a labourer, by night a watchman. There had been a particularly gruesome axe murder in the house and nobody wanted the job. Ashoka needed a roof over his head so was more than happy to oblige. There were two schools of thought anyway about the murder. It might have been a madman in the neighbourhood running riot with an axe; but the victim had been a sitting tenant in the house, so it was more than likely the syndicate was responsible. If so, Ashoka was safe. Nothing like being employed by the murderers themselves. More to the point his employers were safe with him. An Asian without a visa was guaranteed trouble-free: he did what he was told, he was at your beck and call. He was your creature.

None of the workers ever saw any member of the syndicate. Every once in a while a chocolate-coloured Rolls with smoked windows slowed down by the site.

"There you go," Jason would say, but the moment they looked up the car sped on.

"God, I wish I was one of them!" Jason said wistfully.

Ashoka went back to his hole. He was down four feet now, still no drain. If you could find the existing Victorian sewer you could connect your new system to it and save yourself weeks of extra work and money. It made a big difference to Sonny the subcontractor; none at all to Ashoka since he was daily-paid.

It was some time later that he felt the tip of a boot between his shoulder blades and a pleasurable shiver ran down his spine. He looked up to see a tall woman – she looked tall at that angle – with short blond hair.

"Hi there! Diana Frame, Bollingbroke Estates. I've come to measure up."

"Measure up?"

"The house," she said patiently.

"Oh, you're from the syndicate?"

"Syndicate? I've been instructed by the owners. They've given me sole agency of house and contents. Two percent commission."

"Then you have sole agency over me," he replied, "because I come with the contents."

"Two percent of you," she said thoughtfully. "Which two percent were you thinking of?"

"Mrs. Frame," Sonny called from the front door. "They just phoned to say you were on your way. Come on in."

Saturday morning Ashoka got up early. The water in the house was turned off at the mains but there was a tap in the cellar. Filling up a bucket he brought it upstairs, had a wash, then shaved himself in a scrap of mirror propped up on a scaffold board. He got into his school trousers, which still fitted, and a blue shirt. He looked like a schoolboy. It was depressing.

Saturday was surgery day for the local MP on Clapham High Street. Ashoka had his three page letter ready, carefully written out on lined paper. Fifteen closely argued reasons why he should stay in this wonderful country. He didn't quite manage to make it out of the house before the workers arrived so there were catcalls and wolf whistles when he did.

The MP sat in a glass cage, a smoking cigarette in his nicotine-stained fingers. He wore a hearing aid.

"I've been here since the age of eleven!" Ashoka shouted. "I've never been on the dole! All I want to do is lead a decent life!"

"You don't have to shout," the MP said good-naturedly. "I'll see what I can do."

An appeal could take months. In the meantime he was banned – ha! – from doing any work whatsoever. Walking back up the High Street he peeped in through the window of Bollingbroke Estates. Mrs. Frame was bent over the photocopy machine. He didn't go in: he felt embarrassed. He was too well dressed.

Every other evening after work Jason and he walked down to the gym. It was quite a distance, down Acre Lane where the wind whistled through the gaps in the bombed out buildings, past Brixton, and on through the badlands of the Loughborough Estate. It gave him a curious sense of peace, of power, walking through this desolate wasteland which resonated so strongly with the black-and-white wasteland of his mind, that strange amoral landscape he and his mates inhabited. Sometimes though, he saw himself as a point of colour beeping on this monochrome screen, seeking the heat of a like-minded point: a point it never seemed able to find.

They were all there, his usual crowd: Ross and Doug who ran the timber yard, and burned it down every five years for the insurance; gentle Rowan the scaffolder who had just finished doing time for murder; Adam the bodybuilder who threw tenants out of upstair windows for a living. Jason, of course, whose highest aim in life was to drive a chocolate-coloured Rolls with smoked windows; and if there was an axe murder or two along the way who could help it?

In the kingdom of the morally blind, Ashoka thought exultantly, I am the one-eyed king. I am supremely strong.

"That Mrs. Frame," Jason said as they walked back. "Bit of all right, ain't she?"

They parted company at Brixton Town Hall, Jason to take the bus up the Hill to his Mauritian girl. Ashoka walked home alone.

It was a clear cold night. The house brooded in darkness. Ashoka let himself in and immediately felt the slight warmth exuded by the cut pieces of three-by-two lying about and the sawdust on the floor. He went through to the back to use the outside privy. There were some slates missing on its roof and he could see the stars twinkling at him.

Upstairs he brushed his teeth in the remains of the water in the bucket. Then he lit the gas oven that accompanied him from site to site. He unrolled his sleeping bag as close as he could to its open door. Before he snuggled in he looked around. If he died tonight there was nothing, nothing left behind he

could really call his own: and he glowed in the power
of that knowledge.

*   *   *

Mrs. Frame visited the site quite a few times the
following week, stopping by for a chat.

"Have you taken up residence inside that hole?
Because if you stay any longer I might be forced to
start charging you rent."

Another time she pointed to the house with a
long pearly fingernail: "How do you manage to live
in there?"

"Easily," he smiled, "very easily."

Then the drain appeared, miraculously, the
snout of its salt-glazed brown pipe emerging from the
mud like some wicked Victorian crocodile. It was
time to crack open the champagne. At least its
building site equivalent, the PG Tips. They sat all in a
row on a scaffold board supported by paint pots at
either end.

"Good lad." Sonny patted him on the back.
"Now you have to dig round it, real careful."

Once that was done Sonny would slice off the
top with an angle grinder and call in the Drains
Inspector to do a smoke or water test, to ensure the
old pipe was *shitworthy*. It was easy enough to cheat at
this point to get the right result. The important thing
was to have an existing drain to work with, to
connect to.

They worked late to get it ready for the DI in the morning. No sooner had Sonny's beat-up Volvo disappeared down the road than a figure appeared in the dark at the garden gate.

"I've been waiting hours for that man to go," she complained. She was in the same boots she had worn that first day and she was carrying a half-pint bottle of brandy. It was nearly empty.

"You have to help me."

"What's wrong?" he asked.

"Man trouble."

Her eyes were smudged, her voice slurred.

"Come inside," he said taking her hand. But she looked up at the house and shuddered.

"You come with me," she whispered. They drove away in her little red car, across the Common with its pin-points of light, to Lavender Hill on the other side, to the pink conversion flat she lived in. She showed him upstairs into the sitting room with its pink chairs, its pink curtains.

Then she laid him down on the Chinese carpet with its cut-pile pink flowers and proceeded to extract her two percent with gentle, tender greed.

The mornings were always the problem, shivering at the bus stop for the thirty-seven to Clapham Common. Then the mad dash to site to put the kettle on before the others arrived at seven forty-five. He didn't see her every night, he rationed himself. Mondays, Wednesdays and Fridays were for Jason and the gym, then back to the site because he was site watchman after all. The rest were pink nights, and weekends of course.

It gave him a sense of quiet enjoyment leaving his muddy work clothes at her door together with his amorality, to suspend his disbelief one night at a time, to enter this middle-class world of boeuf bourguignon and theatre tickets, the Clarice Cliff in the display cabinet and the talk of what Geraldine James said only this morning when she came in to office to buy a house. Sundays they stayed in bed all day, dozing and making love alternately, eating fry-ups in bed to the thump, thump of Frankie Goes To Hollywood hammering away in the next room. And in the evenings, Art Malik in Jewel In The Crown: because he was the dish du jour back then and all her friends so wanted a hot young Asian for themselves, and wasn't she the lucky one?

Diana had thrown out the previous man, a young surveyor, for being unfaithful. They had been together three years and he wanted to come back. Ashoka couldn't imagine being with anyone three years, it seemed such a long time. The ex was hounding her with phone calls.

One night there was a crash outside and a shout.

The young surveyor was standing on the pavement outside, swaying. He held in his hand the broken handle of the pint glass he had smashed against the side of the house.

"Come out you dirty black bastard," he yelled, "I'll shoot your knee caps off!"

Diana and he cuddled in the dark, giggling.

*   *   *

The drain passed with flying colours. The DI was under the impression he was testing the whole system, but Sonny had judiciously blocked the pipe with a hidden plug a couple of feet further on from the u-tube testing apparatus, far enough down the drain to be out of reach of the DI's wandering hands. They knew they were fairly safe because no DI likes to put his hands into shit anyway. The water level in the tube held admirably.

"Those Victorians," the DI said proudly, "they really knew how to do things back then."

"Naturally," said Sonny.

They had a cup of tea after the DI left to steady their shattered nerves. (The drain was riddled with holes: it had failed miserably only an hour before when they tested it themselves.)

There was no word yet from the Home Office, but Ashoka's illegal alien status raised his stock immeasurably down the gym. Added to that he was bedding this glamorous older woman, quite out of his league.

"Lucky bastard!" Jason said, and you couldn't get a higher compliment than that. His perfect half-hour was far from over.

"There's this wedding," Diana said.

"What wedding?"

"My niece, my brother's daughter. But you don't have to come, really you don't."

"When is it?"

"Next Saturday."

He would have to take the day off. "I'd like to come," he said.

"Really? Are you sure?"

She had always been mysterious about her family. He knew she had a son and daughter of her own. Ashoka was probably closer in age to them than to her.

They drove down early Saturday morning to Eastbourne, to the B & B she had booked, with its overblown furnishings, its rather elderly carpet in the bathroom: all the shabby damp melancholy of the English seaside in autumn. After church they gathered for the reception in a large low room over a pub. They sat at top table with the bride's father and his young dolly-bird mistress. At the other end, as far away as possible, sat the bride's mother.

There were speeches.

"I remember my own wedding rather well," said the bride's father. "I saw this dirty great nose coming up the aisle, and attached to it was your mother. So I turned to my best man and said, "Get me a brandy. And quick."

Then the bride's mother took her turn at the mike. She began reading out a poem, mostly addressed to the young bridegroom.

"I remember the day he left," she began,

"I cried and I cried and I cried.

So be good to my daughter or else, young man,
I'll cry and I'll cry and I'll cry."

There was more in the same vein. Quite a lot
more. Then the mother blew her nose loudly into the
microphone and shuffled off, overcome by the
magnificence of her own words.

"Jesus!" said the father. "I remember now why I
left her. But you know, she's gone from bad to verse."

Afterwards he spoke to Ashoka, chewing
thoughtfully on a small cigar.

"You're a hell of a lot better than the last one," he
said. "I never liked that little tosser."

They trooped outside together to throw confetti
at the happy couple.

"Bloody better look after my car or you'll be in
trouble," he growled at his newly acquired son-in-law.
The young couple got in.

It was a chocolate Rolls with smoked windows.

The hairs on Ashoka's neck began to rise. He felt
his head spin. The father turned back to him as the
car roared off.

"You're doing a fine job there on those drains,"
he said. "Keep up the good work, son."

* * *

Ashoka waited till the drive back to say anything.

"Why didn't you tell me about your brother and
the syndicate?"

"Look," she replied quickly, "what he does is his business. They just retain me to sell their properties, OK?"

He looked at her. "No," he said despairingly, "not OK. Can't you see how you've put yourself in his power, become his creature?"

"Creature? That's bloody rich," she replied. "What does that make you? Who do you think pays *your* wages?"

But his blame in the matter seemed to him somehow less: he was, after all, very much lower down the food chain than she was. He thought with regret of her pretty, pink kingdom and all it had meant to him these past few months: it had been his oasis, his refuge, from the petty crookery of his small-time builder's world. A fool's paradise, he thought grimly, but I can taste the poison now, the bitter chocolate at its heart.

She tried to explain to him how it was not that simple: how too often life was only a set of tired, shabby compromises all the way to the grave: not everyone could afford the luxury of his very high-minded principles. But she realized he was too young to understand. Not now, not today.

"Anyway," she said, "it's not as if we get to pick our brothers and sisters. We're not that lucky."

"Then I am indeed blessed," he replied bitterly, "because I have no one."

She put her hand gently on his thigh to comfort him in his great sadness, but he ignored it, and after a while she took it away. The damp air hung between them like a curtain.

"Everything I have is for us," she said softly. "We could be so good together." The chairs, the carpet, the curtains: she was offering him the very pink of her existence.

But I will die, he thought. He felt suddenly tired, old, no longer strong. Go back to your surveyor, he wanted to say, he's so much more deserving than I will ever be. Somehow, somewhere, the long hand of the clock had crept past the half-hour and he hadn't even noticed.

*   *   *

Back on site Monday morning there was a letter for him in a brown envelope, OHMS. He scanned its contents.

"...given leave to enter for an indefinite period... Present your passport for processing at the Home Office, Lunar House, Wellesley Road ....."

He was legal at last!

So what, exactly, did he feel?

And the answer to that was: nothing. Absolutely nothing. He was the foetus in the fluid, floating, almost motionless, unaffected by this great sound and fury all around. Was it as yet unborn? Was it already dead and pickled? You couldn't really say, you didn't really know.

Then a funny thing happened, a miracle almost. The eyes fluttered open. Get a life, they seemed to say, get real.

It was all very much like in a B-movie.

* * *

The grey-carpeted stairway was just the same, and upstairs the two girls still at it like express trains. Nothing had changed. But for him it was almost a lifetime later.

She looked up. "Oh it's you," she said.

"I got my residency," he replied.

"The Home Office has already informed us."

"But that's not what I came about."

"Yes?" The eyes looked at him mercilessly through their horizontal frames.

"What I mean is...what I wanted to say...will you be free to have a drink with me one of these evenings?"

She looked at him coolly, in silence. And for a moment there his future hung, teetering crazily in the balance. There was no dirt under his finger nails.

"There's a pub three doors down," she said. "Six o'clock. Don't be late."

Maybe, he thought with a slight quickening of the heart, *maybe the jack fruit is not too far gone yet.*

Last Man Standing

The Admiral watched the woman in the blue tee shirt feeding her two children. She was cutting up bacon for the younger one. The elder boy was flicking corn flakes around the open pavilion that served as the hotel dining room. It was too early in the morning for children. The Admiral looked glumly down at his plate of sticky rice and curried tuna. He was a very important person: he wore national dress at all times, the white tunic, the white sarong, so it was only natural the hotel should choose to honour him with an ethnic breakfast; all the same the bacon smelt wonderful. But noblesse *will* oblige, and the Admiral ploughed on through his glutens.

He could hear the manager of the hotel. "We are very pleased to have you back with us yet again this Christmas," he was saying to the woman. "How many years has it been in all?"

"Fourteen," she replied.

"Enjoy your meal."

With great dignity the manager removed a corn flake from his ear and retired, avoiding the Admiral's table altogether.

The little boy burped. The woman giggled and the Admiral stood up sharply, his chair falling back in outraged sympathy. Just then the sunlight in the pavilion began to dim – somebody was trying to turn it down so the real performance of the day could begin – and right on cue the wave appeared in the far corner of the dining room, the roaring grey ghost at the Boxing Day feast.

The elder boy was the first to react. He sprang up and faced the wave in a half-crouch. Then he hurled his bowl of cornflakes at it. The woman screamed. Instinctively she put her arm around the younger boy. The older one ran towards her, and she gripped his hand thinking, please God may I be able to hold on to them both. The head of the younger boy went under and with a supreme effort she managed to lift him above the surface of the water, realising as she did with a flicker of karmic sadness that her grip on the other boy had weakened.

"Amma!" he said with a look of mild reproach on his face. He was swept away in a sea of tables and chairs, cups and plates, all the detritus of a five-star hotel breakfast. That single word he spoke, the look he gave, would come back again and again to haunt her in the sleepless long night of the rest of her life.

With a nimbleness born of years in the political arena, the Admiral leapt lightly onto a passing pettagama. He couldn't help noticing it was rather a fine chest, late seventeenth-century Dutch, of flowered satinwood. It was quite seaworthy, really. Clipping his mobile to his ear to call for reinforcements, the Admiral floated smartly down past reception and out into open country. It was, he thought, rather like being back in the Navy again.

The woman found herself wedged in the branches of a tree, her younger son clinging to her leg below. The rough bark felt strangely comforting and she put her bruised face against it. She had swallowed so much mud and seawater she felt as if all the ills of the world were within her. There was no sign of the other boy. She saw a figure floating towards her, its milky cataracted eyes staring ahead, its grey hair spread out in a fan behind.

"Over here!" she cried, "I'm over here!"

But it was only a corpse on a log, drifting by, wide-eyed and serene on its last journey home.

The woman looked about her, at the empty sea, the cruel sky. She thought of all the things left unsaid and undone in her life: she closed her eyes, and was so very sorry.

Then the second wave struck.

A single chopper flapped in the sky – an unwieldy bird of prey looking for carrion – and three Pajeros raced to the preordained piece of high ground where it landed, offering up their choice morsel of humankind. Then they roared away again. And if they didn't seem to hear the moans of the bodies struggling in the mud all around, perhaps it was because their tinted windows were up and their air-conditioning was on.

From his seat high up in the air, the Admiral looked down on the lashing curly-wurly sea below.

All men are born to die, he thought, with genuine regret. He clipped the buckle of his seatbelt tight, placing his fingertips precisely on it.

But some men sooner than others, *some sooner than others*.

The woman sat on the steps of the hospital where they had brought her with her younger son. Every time a lorry drove in, she ran to it screaming. The bodies were toppled off gently onto an ever-growing pile. I made the wrong decision, she thought, how much better if we had all died in this together. But she hadn't died: she had been left to live, with the far more difficult task of grieving.

As daylight faded and her hopes dissolved into the sooty blackness of dusk, the last lorry rolled in. But there were only more bodies on it. She turned to go when the passenger door of the cab opened and a small figure slid wordlessly to the ground.

It was really too dark to see his face though she didn't have to. She could well imagine the look of mild reproach on it.

The Moon Princess

The phone jangled as Ganesh left the house. He pressed the button:

"Clean jeans," it read. "Ironed shirt." Ganesh threw the phone into the back of the car and reversed out onto busy Duplication Road.

Ganga's messages were always terse and to the point. Ganesh usually ignored them. This time though, he actually was in a spotless white shirt. The jeans were rather faded but Ganga was not to know that.

Every few months Ganga arrived from Australia with her reformist tendencies to the fore, scattering sweetness and light as she fondly imagined, leaving Ganesh and Apapa to reap the chaos and confusion she left behind. It usually took them months to recover. If only she would give them a little notice before she arrived! But she never did. Apapa was even thinking of applying to the World Bank for funds to set up an early warning system.

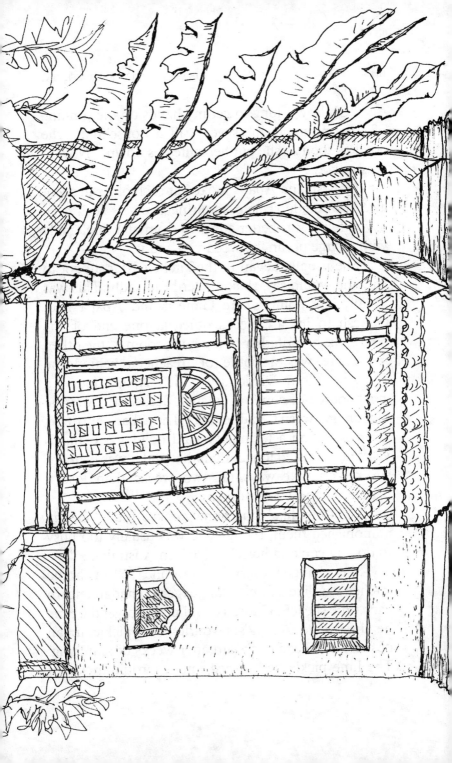

"Oh how I long to get my hands on the running of this miserable mess you call a household," she cried as soon as she put her suitcases down. "Now in Australia. . ."

Ganesh and Apapa looked at each other in silent awe. You couldn't help admiring Ganga's zeal, even if you felt it was better admired from afar, preferably with a large ocean between you and it.

She usually began in the kitchen. "It's all got to go," she would say, shaking her head sadly. This was usually the point where Ganesh and Apapa fled, Ganesh to his architect's office at one end of the house, his grandfather to the book-room at the other.

There was a bottle of Teacher's behind the Shorter Oxford Dictionary which Apapa found a great source of comfort on such occasions. And the dictionary wasn't bad either. They had hurriedly given Letchimi a fortnight's paid holiday – Ganga's visits never lasted longer than that and it was better to survive on takeaways for two weeks than lose a perfectly good cook-woman.

"Nothing like good home-cooked food," Ganga admonished them, though she was usually too busy to do any cooking herself. "Now in Australia. . ."

She changed everything around so much the kitchen was like a foreign language you had to relearn each time she left. Ganesh could never forget the time he discovered Apapa's favourite lime-pickle in an obscure overhead cupboard after weeks of searching. The lime pickle had turned into a terrible trickle of slime. It nearly said *Vanakkam* to him and walked out of the kitchen on its own two legs.

The traffic on Duplication road was horrendous day or night. Ganesh manoeuvred carefully past the fevered commerce at the House of Passions, then on through the toxic treats of Thunmulla Junction at rush-hour. Ganga had come to Sri Lanka this time on a special mission.

"High time you got married and settled down," she told him. "It's not as if I'm getting any younger." Ganesh forbore to mention that he and Apapa were quite happy as they were, thank you very much, and since when did his sister getting older have anything to do with it? But he played along for the sake of peace, as you do when you're charming and all you want is the quiet life. On her last visit Ganga had taken him to a shady Maradana man in dark glasses who read his palm.

"I can see a mango tree outside your future home," he said, "and a long line of cars stretching all the way down the road." Ganesh was surprised he could see anything at all his glasses were so dark.

"I'm getting married to the daughter of a fruit-eating car-salesman," he told Apapa when he got home.

"Very good," Apapa retorted with spirit. "That way I'll have more people to cadge lifts off in future."

This time round Ganga had fixed him up to see a rather glamorous and esoteric tarot card reader in de Saram Place, and that was where he was headed now.

Ganesh steered the car past the vast emporium that was Odel with its gigantic cut-outs of happy, smiling *Odelpeople*, looming large over little bronze Sir Charles with the crow crapping on his head. Then on past the aluminium pails of anthuriums on Dean's Road: with their oversize, lipstick-pink lacquered heads which dropped off no sooner you got them home and into water. He turned into de Saram Place at the corner of the Eye Hospital when the phone rang again.

"Forget Miss Tarot," it read, "come to Taj Lobby. Excellent prospect."

At this point, the car gave an elegant little shudder and cut out. Ganesh coasted silently along, past the row of stationary cars on de Saram Place, coming to a stop, almost fortuitously it seemed, at a makeshift open air garage underneath a spreading tree. There was a lot of banging and hammering in progress on various overturned three-wheelers. It all looked suspiciously like someone's award-winning installation art.

He was immediately surrounded by a riot of mechanics.

"It's your plugs," said one.

"It's your points," said another.

"I'd have to look at your brake-linings," said a third, more creative one.

Directly at the back of all this invigorating open air theatre Ganesh could see the blue gates of the tarot card reader's house.

"How long will it take?"

The mechanics shook their collective head.

"I'm running late," Ganesh pleaded, "I'm supposed to be at the Taj Hotel even now."

"I should think an hour at least," said one.

"Maybe two?" queried another.

"You can collect your car tomorrow," said the creative one.

"I don't care what you do and how badly you do it. Just get the damn thing started, and quick."

At this there were ugly murmurs of dissent. It was quite accepted you had to do a shoddy job now and then. But there was absolutely no excuse for speed.

Ganesh threw them the keys with the casual violence of a bride throwing a bouquet at a group of hungry bridesmaids. He strode up to the blue gates and as he did his phone rang again. "Dark trousers," it warned, "white shirt."

Ganesh unlatched the gate and walked up to the front door where he rang the bell.

The door opened to reveal a woman in flowing flowered gown. She stood before him in a severe backward sloping stance, ready for any eventuality, the guardian at the gates.

"I am the mother of the Moon Princess," she announced.

"And I am Ganesh."

"You're late, that's what you are."

Ganesh explained about the car.

"Oh don't get me started on those mechanics out there. Clinking clanking all day long. I've complained and complained to the Municipality but it's no good. It's that shady tree I blame. Cut it! I said to the Moon Princess, Cut it! But she won't listen, will she? It's a mango tree, she says, life-giving, she says. That's the trouble with the Moon Princess, you see, she's so ecological…" The voice tapered off uncertainly.

"Now that I'm here do you think I could have a reading?" Ganesh made as if to come in but she blocked his way.

"Oh you can't come in *here* – you have to go round that side, through *her* entrance. Only I am allowed this way."

Ganesh could see her through the vertical lines of the window bars as he went round the side of the house. The Moon Princess sat, like a cat in a birdcage, inscrutably beautiful. She was licking her paw. On closer inspection this proved to be an ice cream she was holding in her hand.

"It's this heat," she explained. She licked the last of the ice cream and flicked the cone away, Ganesh watching with regret its expert arc into the bin.

She motioned for Ganesh to sit, and began shuffling an oversize pack of cards with the sort of disdainful professional elegance you associate with croupiers. But Ganesh could still see vertical lines around her, almost invisible, as if she were in a cage, and he blinked to clear his eyes.

"Cut," she commanded.

"Coffee?" asked a querulous voice through the door, "Tea?"

"Go away, mother, I'm working," said the Moon Princess, a little sharply.

"Do you ever read your own fortune?" Ganesh asked curiously.

"Funny thing, I'm the one person I don't seem to be able to do. I find my own thought processes interfere with the interpretation."

The Moon Princess spread the cards out in a fan. "Pick thirteen."

Ganesh could hear the mother's voice outside on the phone.

"Get me the Ambassador," she was saying. "He'll be very angry with you if you don't put me through straightaway." Her voice was no longer querulous or unsure.

The Moon Princess looked long and hard at the thirteen overturned cards but remained silent. Ganesh couldn't help noticing she had beautiful fingers.

"Ah, Ambassador, finally! I have the Moon Princess here in Colombo on a flying visit, yes. . She's on her way to Hong Kong, yes. I find she has a little window tomorrow between 7.25 and 7.45. . .Yes, I know it's early in the morning, yes. Shall I pencil you in?"

The Moon Princess collected the cards together and shuffled again. Once more she began to examine the thirteen Ganesh selected. His phone rang and he started guiltily.

"Turn it off!" She was beginning to sound a little tetchy, he thought. She continued looking at the cards but it didn't seem to help. "I'm sorry," she said finally, "it must be one of my off days."

As if to spare her further embarrassment there was a timid knock on the door.

"Your car's ready," said the quavering voice from the other side, "I've got the keys...."

Outside, Ganesh checked his messages: There were two.

The first said: "Taj totally unsuitable. Plenty more fish.."

The second said: "Now in Australia..."

But Ganesh had great difficulty getting his car out. Maybe it was the thin skein of lines all around him which just wouldn't go away however much he blinked.

Then again maybe it was the line of cars stretching all the way down, from the mango tree to the end of the road.

Pig

"Has he arrived yet?" Lalitha asked the receptionist at the counter.

"No, but he called to say he'll be here by five-thirty this evening."

She didn't have to explain who she was talking about. She and Ruwan had been coming to this same hotel so long they were virtually part of its fixtures and fittings.

"Five-thirty? Not long to wait then." She picked up the overnight case and made her way upstairs.

ৡ   ৡ   ৡ

They had lived down the road from each other as children. Every day they walked home from school hand in hand; they were childhood sweethearts, they were best friends. And when they came of age, in the time-honoured Sri Lankan tradition they were given in marriage. To other people.

In Sri Lanka the people you lived amongst, the people you went to school with, the people in whose houses you ate, whose jokes you shared: these were not the people you married. Quite possibly they were not your religion. More to the point they were probably not your caste. This word with its fearsome connotations was never, hardly ever, used. But it was ever present: it muddied the waters of Sri Lanka's politics, it perfumed the air of her bed-chambers; it lurked, like a particularly noxious relative, behind the poruwa of every wedding ceremony. It was the c-word. People used its synonym, its acronym, its antonym – indeed any other nym that came to mind – in the vain hope its meaning would somehow go away. It didn't.

But if the people you chose to associate with were the very ones you could not marry, then the ones you did marry were quite often people you wouldn't dream of associating with if you had any choice in the matter. Lalitha was given in marriage to an extremely wealthy Sri Lankan who owned a large hospital in West Palm Beach, Florida.

His character was larger than life, he had large appetites, he was large. Ruwan was married off to a Kandyan princess of obscure name, with bloodlines as long as your arm, whose genealogy had to compensate somehow for a whole host of relatives living in discreet penury in the less beautiful parts of New Jersey. If indeed any part of New Jersey can be called beautiful. So by force of circumstance, good fortune, karma, call it what you will, both ended up in America.

It was a case of infidelity waiting to happen.

But they never met in America. Every year the week before Christmas they met briefly, a day or two at most, in room two hundred and three of Brown's Beach Hotel, Negombo. They had been meeting this way for nineteen years.

But how different this year! Four months back her husband had keeled over and died, in the very hospital he owned.

They were having dinner at home when he felt the tightening in his chest. She liked to cook him dinner every evening, the chop and chips arranged prettily on the plate, the salad on the side with its ranch dressing. It was one of the things she adored about living in the West, how you could make such an expert-looking meal in the time it took back home to scrape a coconut.

He laughed at her efforts. "Throw this crap away," he said, "let's go out." And frequently they did. But she liked this little effort she expended every evening. It was a discipline. It gave her pleasure to satisfy his vast and varied appetites: even if what she had on offer was frequently not enough. She never forgot the American girl who appeared at their front door one Saturday morning. Lalitha could still picture her, in her short – very short – tennis dress, framed by the columns of the porch with the slip-slap of the Atlantic Ocean behind.

"I've come to play with your husband," she said.

Lalitha slammed the door shut. There were tears and recriminations; but finally it had all ended in laughter. It always did because her husband was nothing if not funny.

"Throw this crap away," he said and then he keeled over. She thought now with regret of his generosity, his open-handedness. She had rushed him to his own hospital, but too late.

There was a knock on the door and her heart gave a jolt, as it always did, every year, and in a moment Ruwan had wrapped her up in his arms, squeezing her tight.

"God, how I missed you."

She could get the faint smell of soap on him – he never used aftershave – and feel his rangy body underneath the shirt, so different from her husband's.

"Stand back, let me look at you."

She could see the finely drawn face, now showing its lines, the salt and pepper hair.

"I heard," he said, "I'm so very sorry."

She had not called him: she knew the news would get to him soon enough through the Sri Lankan bush telegraph, widespread as it was and better established than any satellite transmission.

"I've spent the last few months sorting out his effects. I sold out to the other directors."

"Then you're a very rich woman," he said softly.

She laughed. "So what next?"

He didn't answer. He was thinking of his own wife the Kandyan princess, now grown a little stout with age but still rather charming. They had escaped New Jersey, shaken loose from her rather clinging family and made it to Manhattan. They had been lucky with the three bed flat in Thompson Street, SoHo – bought from the American poet who had taken a fancy to his wife – worth nothing then, worth an enormous amount now.

He worked at NYU, just up the road in Washington Square, in the accounts department.

It was a part of New York unspoilt enough to remind him of the gracious world of Edith Wharton.

No, he thought, I haven't done too badly either. Then he remembered his often repeated promise to Lalitha and his thoughts came back to the present.

ৼ ৼ ৼ

They could hear the ceaseless wail of the Indian Ocean below, the waves prostrating themselves on the beach one after the other, dragged back mercilessly into the sea each time.

Lalitha slept, and as she slept she dreamt. She dreamt of Coconut Grove the first time she saw it on a Saturday night, the crowds on the redbrick sidewalks, the flashy red Corvettes in line, driven by girls in white boob tubes, honey coloured hair on honey coloured shoulders. The very next Saturday she had been back in a white boob tube of her own, and a skirt with purple parrots and yellow palm trees all over. She still had that skirt, it still fitted; she wore it on special occasions. Her husband had not bought her the Corvette though. He had bought her a Mercedes Sports instead.

She sighed in her sleep, and as she slept Ruwan watched. With her hair spread out extravagantly on the pillow underneath like a feathered headdress she looked more like a princess than his own wife; and for the umpteenth time he thought: What if? What if?

"What?" she asked. Her eyes had opened and she was watching him watching her.

"I want to take you away," he said softly. "Can you spare three days?"

She made a quick calculation. Her brothers were not expecting her for another two, and anyway they were used to the vagaries of her schedule. As long as she was "back" for Christmas it was enough.

They came down next morning to be greeted by a very grimy fifteen-seater bus with scraps of cloth fluttering at the windows.

"Are you sure we have enough room?" she asked.

"Best I could do at short notice," he said shrugging his shoulders, slightly annoyed at her facetiousness. She wondered why he hadn't hired an ordinary taxi. Perhaps it would have been more costly.

He saw she was dressed in a strange skirt of purple parrots and yellow palm trees, and thought of his own wife, who might not have been blessed in the looks department but who had an almost unerring eye for what was right or wrong on any occasion.

"We're in a quiet neighbourhood here," he said. "Are you sure that skirt is allowed?"

She laughed, though he knew somehow she had not got the joke.

The driver was wiping a square foot of grime from the windows with a very small cloth. There were many more square feet to go.

"Meet Mr. Nilwala," Ruwan said.

Mr. Nilwala extended a lugubrious hand for Lalitha to shake. It felt like something he had recently picked up in the Negombo Fish Market.

"I'm taking you to Nuwara Eliya," Ruwan told her. He turned to Mr. Nilwala.

"Through Gampola or Ratnapura?"

"Ratnapura."

"Isn't Gampola quicker?"

"My wife," said Mr. Nilwala. He paused sadly. "Lives in Ratnapura. Very ill."

They went through Ratnapura.

It was the first trip they were taking together in all their nineteen years. In Negombo they always stayed inside the hotel room: outside they would have been recognised immediately: Negombo was, after all, only a curious sort of concrete village by the sea where everyone knew everyone else. They were taking so much time off together it was almost like being man and wife.

The bus came to a juddering halt at the cool spot near Kottawa.

"It's all right," Ruwan told the driver, "we don't need breakfast. You can drive on."

Breakfast in America was only a snatched cup of coffee; that's all they were used to.

Mr. Nilwala turned round and looked at them.

"You must be hungry," Ruwan said. "Please. Go on in, have something, we're in no hurry. We'll wait in the bus."

Mr. Nilwala continued looking, mutely, dolefully.

So they all went in and had breakfast. They didn't mind, it was a holiday after all.

Ruwan watched her eating stringhoppers with her fingers and for some reason his fastidious nature was aroused. Nineteen years away had made him forget the use of his fingers but Lalitha ate like a local, as if she had never left. Afterwards she sucked her fingers clean with a sort of feline thoroughness that left him disgusted and attracted in equal measure.

But there was more to it than that. It was really as if in the nineteen years away she had become more native than the natives: a textbook Sri Lankan almost, who had unaccountably failed to notice that Sri Lanka itself had quietly moved on in her absence.

With her big hair, her colourful skirt, she had become somehow a white man's idea of a native. But in that case, he thought rather ruefully, what am I, in my buttoned down shirt and my tasselled loafers? Aren't I just a native's idea of a white man?

It was difficult, there were no clear answers. He thought of the tea bush, existing for thousands of years in China as a straggling plant in poor soil, capable only of producing the weak infusion they called green tea; then one fine day the Brits brought it to places like Nuwara Eliya where it positively flourished, producing an entirely different drink. Which then was the real tea?

Perhaps this is what the West has done to us both, he thought, turned us into caricatures of ourselves; unmistakeably genuine, yet not at all the real thing.

They reached Ratnapura and some way past town Mr. Nilwala negotiated the bus with difficulty into a roadside clearing. There was a small house, and a woman bounded out beaming.

"My sick wife," said Mr. Nilwala sadly.

They were served the statutory cups of over-milked over-sugared tea in white irridescent china, and Lalitha slurped hers in the traditional manner. Ruwan almost stepped back expecting her to spit out on the floor like some arcane tea-tasting expert.

Further on Mr. Nilwala stopped at a misty waterfall.

"A misty waterfall," he noted gloomily.

"We're in a bit of a hurry. We'd like to get to Nuwara Eliya before dark."

Mr. Nilwala turned the engine off. He took the key out.

They got down and had a look at the misty waterfall.

It was raining in Nuwara Eliya. The Grand Hotel greeted them with all the charm of a dowager with bronchitis, but they were happy. It was almost like being on honeymoon, the honeymoon before the wedding. He had always promised her the day her husband died he would leave his wife and marry her. Maybe tomorrow, she thought happily as she drifted off to sleep, maybe tomorrow he'll ask.

ھ ھ ھ

She came down to breakfast next morning in a black sari worked all over in gold, high black stilettos and a gold evening bag.

"We're only going to World's End," he said eyeing her doubtfully. "There's lots of walking to do."

"Please," she urged, "it's my only chance of getting some good pictures with you. I've dressed for the pictures."

He looked troubled but said nothing.

They drove to World's End, forty-five minutes away, along with several hundred other people who had decided that a visit there that morning was a must.

Ruwan said to Mr. Nilwala: "Go on back to the hotel, put your feet up, relax. As long as you're back here to pick us up by five this evening it's enough."

Mr. Nilwala glowered at them silently for a full minute. Then he drove off.

They joined the nature trail with the other hundred odd couples, all young, all part of Sri Lanka's emerging eco-army, laughing and yelling at the tops of their voices, throwing sweet wrappers into bushes, snapping twigs off trees. There was this peculiarly Sri Lankan notion that in the wilderness no silence was ever to be left unfilled, no flower unplucked: there was great danger to society leaving so much beauty unchecked. Back in the concrete jungles of the city there was very little beauty so no such danger; and people were much better behaved.

"Let's get away from all this," she said turning off the path.

Suddenly the voices faded away.

"Are you sure you're doing the right thing?" he asked anxiously.

"Trust me," she smiled.

They struck off across a wide open rolling plain covered in bracken and gorse, and though he had never been to Scotland he imagined this must be what a grouse moor must look like; but it reminded *her* of the Florida everglades, which she crossed once a fortnight on her way to their holiday bungalow on the other coast, on the Gulf of Mexico.

"How's your wife?" she asked. "Does she go to work now your daughter's grown up and left home?"

He shook his head. "She was always very happy to stay at home."

It struck Lalitha how his life had been so much more conventional, so much more grown-up than hers: he had raised a child and put her through school, a rebellious teenager who had left home as soon as she could, marrying the first American boy that came along; he had been plagued by money problems. She had been spared on both counts. She had decided early on not to have children and it had left her free to enjoy a life of almost child-like simplicity. There had been more than enough money, but from the start she had told her husband:

"I want to work, do a job."

"Oh?"

She explained about the job she had been offered: standing about all day inside Burdine's with her little tray of cheese slivers on cocktail sticks, trying to entice customers to have a taste in the hope they would buy the cheese afterwards.

He roared with laughter. "You go, girl!"

She made less in a month than she was accustomed to spend at one time on a single pair of shoes: and the shoes were hers merely for the asking. But it was not the money.

She wanted, no, needed the job, to get herself out of the house, have herself a life. She was not content being just another Sri Lankan trophy wife, buffed and botoxed as they were these days.

He had never denied her anything. He had said yes to everything she ever wanted and been able to provide it. Everything except perhaps love.

They had crossed the open plain now and were back in jungle again. Ruwan looked behind him to see a thin mist floating over the purple ground as if somebody was following them, drawing a slow veil over, covering it from prying eyes.

"This way," she said. He wanted to ask, how do you know? But she seemed so sure he didn't like to question her.

Then they heard it. It was the sound a cistern makes when you flush and the water empties: the musical groan of an empty pipe. It was so peculiar in the stillness of the jungle that neither made any comment.

A few minutes later they heard it again.

"What's that?" he asked and she could see he was worried. "Sounds like a wild boar."

She laughed. "Probably the ghost of my dear dead husband, following us to make sure you don't steal me away. I must say he used to snore just like that. The pig!"

Then they heard it again, closer. They quickened their steps and for the first time she regretted her costume. Her sari fall was slipping down, her heels kept sticking in the mud. She clutched her metallic bag like a gold grenade. Ruwan had long since lost the tassels on his loafers. One of the buttons of his fine tweed jacket dangled by a thread giving him an absurdly comic air, as if a grain of basmati was dangling from his chin.

But in the midst of all this turmoil she was calm. She thought: I have always led my life firmly, by the ring through its nose, never letting it lead me; always been its master, never its slave. My life has gone pretty much where I've wanted it to go. So why should I be worried now?

And suddenly, as if to reward her for such bravado they began to hear through the mist the sound of falling water, and with it the yells and shouts of the Sri Lankan eco-army, and with a sudden gush of relief she saw the discarded half-eaten lunch packets strewn along the path like rose petals. Civilisation!

         ॐ   ॐ   ॐ

Mr. Nilwala was on hand to meet them, fuming quietly. Back at the hotel they told the manager about the wild pig.

"Pig?" he said, "You're joking, aren't you? That was a leopard following you. There are *over seventy* roaming around World's End."

She threw back her head then and roared with laughter, raucously, because she didn't believe a word of it. But Ruwan was silent, it wasn't his idea of a joke. All he could think of was his family back home and how they would have coped if anything happened to him.

The sari was torn in several places and filthy beyond cleaning. She unwound herself and threw it with great satisfaction into the bin. She had her bath.

Tonight, she thought with high good humour, tonight he'll ask.

They went down to dinner and there was a lighted candle on their table, the only one, like some secret signal from the management to congratulate them on their good fortune in getting back alive. They worked their way through dinner: brown Windsor soup, boiled ham and faded green beans, bread pudding: a native's idea of a white man's dinner.

"Lalitha," he began. "We've been meeting like this for what, nineteen years?"

She nodded happily.

"Are you content?"

She nodded again. It was not in her nature to be unhappy. She had always been willing to play the hand she was dealt, good or bad, and she always played to win.

"Is there any sense," he began, choosing his words carefully, "is there any sense trying to change what has worked so well all these years?"

She looked at him then in disbelief, the blood rushing to her head. Two days every year, she wanted to shout, nineteen years! Is that all I have ever been good for? Is that all I ever meant to you? If you're not going to commit now, when you have the chance, did you ever have any intention? Did you? So what in that case have we meant to each other all these years?

He too was thinking. Nineteen years. For two days every year we have been actor and actress in this well-rehearsed play with this well-known ending; but our real selves have moved on, only a fraction each year maybe, but we're actually quite far apart now

aren't we, you with your wild skirt, me with my
brown loafers? We've become highly coloured
caricatures of ourselves. So why not just let it be at
that, let the play go on as it always has?

"Why change?" he repeated out loud.

She looked at him, saying nothing. Then it
struck her.

He's afraid, she thought, *he's afraid!* She
imagined she could see the slight flicker of yellow in
his eyes, but she couldn't be sure, it might have only
been the reflection of the candle flame.

They finished dinner and walked side by side in
silence to the lift; and suddenly, inconsequentially, she
thought of her husband who had never denied her
anything, his generosity, his open-handedness. I
never told him, she thought sadly, how much it all
meant to me, I took it all for granted. All I ever did in
return was cheat on him. Ruwan held the lift doors
open for her.

But as she stepped in, a picture of the girl in the
short tennis dress came floating into her mind out of
nowhere, and with a sudden, silent, *whoosh*, her
spirits soared up, up, up!

Oh, No, Roger, No, No, No,!

Then Jesus asked: "Who did the tiling? A blind man?"

And I replied: "I sacked him this morning."

And I wasn't joking. The tile-work was truly appalling. Just that morning I had sworn to myself I would never tile another bathroom as long as I lived.

Then Jesus said: "We'll take it. We can't afford to wait. The wife is pregnant."

Now I'm perfectly well aware that in the Bible it is Joseph who is house-hunting with Mary who is pregnant with Jesus, but you know us builders, our grasp of Scripture is shaky at the best of times. So we called them Jesus and Mary. He was actually called Jesús, he was Colombian; she had some complicated name which I think meant starlight. Jesús and Starlight? No, it didn't have quite the same ring to it . . .

We were in the middle there of the blue-rinsed Thatcher Eighties, and I was selling these flats as fast

as I could knock them out: carving them out of lovely old Brixton houses which I bought from courteous and civilised elderly black couples who had arrived, back in the Fifties, to work the London buses and underground.

These were selling up now, retiring to the home counties; and from the home counties came my young white buyers, wearing ropes of fat juicy pearls around their neck and calling each other names like Verity or Constance or Faith. It's quite possible those elderly black couples were going off to live right next door to the parents of Verity or Faith or Constance, who would snub them graciously the rest of their lives. The young couples in their turn were likely to be given a very hard time in Brixton, with its polarised attitudes, its high crime rate, its faint air of menace. All in all it seemed a fair trade-off to me.

Being brown I didn't fit into this scheme of things. I was only the builder, I didn't have to. But Jesus and Mary were yellow, they were Colombian, and I never quite figured out how they had managed to fly below the radar to get here, to this troubled part of South London where there was no room for people in the middle, people like us.

I showed them around the ground-floor flat which had splendid high ceilings, a dining room separated from the living by a pair of magnificent panelled double doors, and a small conservatory kitchen. And I was pleased if a little puzzled when they said they would take it.

As it happened the flat on the top floor became occupied first, by a fresh-faced home counties doctor called Roger and his Sloane Ranger wife. He worked at St. Thomas's Hospital and came home sharp at four every afternoon. She stayed in all day. At three forty-five precisely she brought out her dustpan and brush to the front door of her flat.

She could be found on all fours when he arrived, scrubbing vigorously.

"Hard day darling?"

"You know how it is," she would reply, "busy, busy, busy!"

They retired upstairs arm in arm. This was our signal. We raced up for tea-break, to the room directly below their bedroom.

It didn't take long.

The bed rocked, the boards creaked.

There was a small scream.

"Oh no Roger, no, no, no!"

Short and sharp; just like the tea-break.

And quite as invigorating.

Jesus and Mary moved into the ground-floor flat and I moved out my things – all three of them – to the middle floor where work was still going on. Jesus had a job in a small South American travel agency in the West End but Mary worked locally, at a shoe shop in Stockwell. Although she was pregnant it was early days and she still went in every day. The thing about them was that they were so small, so delicately formed, like two miniature dolls, you wondered how they were going to survive in the jungle that was Brixton back then. You couldn't even think of them having a child – it seemed somehow obscene – because they were children themselves.

They invited Sonny and me to dinner that first week. Mary had her mother over from Colombia, a wizened witch-like person with coal-black eyes. You could imagine her in poncho and hat on an Andean hillside, smoking a leisurely cigar, selling brightly coloured root vegetables by the road. You couldn't imagine her in London. You especially couldn't imagine her as the mother of Mary who was round and soft and dewy-complexioned, like a newly opened flower.

"When a man marries," Sonny said to me quite loudly, "he should take a good look at his mother-in-law first, to understand where life will take him."

Sonny was wandering round the flat surreptitiously inspecting all its flaws – the damp patches, the cracks – everything we had so cunningly disguised before the sale.

When you've worked on a house it remains forever your baby – far more than any mere owner who comes after you: you know secrets about it they will go to their grave not knowing.

Jesus and Mary were in the kitchen, and I was left at the dining table to keep the conversational ball rolling.

"How did you get here?" I asked the old lady. "Was it a long flight?"

Sonny was standing behind her astride a broomstick, making flying motions.

Jesus came in with the first course. Fried chicken skins. Sonny made quite a loud retching noise. The old lady just sat there, placidly devouring her food. There was chicken Stroganoff to follow, and afterwards, instead of pudding Mary asked: "Do you want to see my emeralds?"

It was not the sort of question you said no to, and she brought out a long brown velvet box. There were dozens of them, chips really, tiny and exquisitely set, rather like Mary herself.

"Are they insured?" I asked, thinking of the area we lived in, the muggings, the burglaries.

"They're not all that valuable," she said. "But they're extremely dear to me."

(((

Every day mid-morning we went off for breakfast to Mandy's caff, under the arches at Clapham North: fried eggs and bacon; sausages and tomatoes and beans; and mushrooms and fried bread. And chips of course, every day. Followed by Mandy's cherry pie and ice cream. Did I ever tell you about my slight cholesterol problem?

It was after one of these deeply fulfilling breakfasts that we came back to find the door to Jesus and Mary's flat forced open. I poked my head round.

"Don't go in," Sonny warned. We called Mary at work and she arrived within ten minutes. There was no point calling the police. There were so many burglaries in the area they rarely paid house-calls. Mary came out of the flat weeping.

"My emeralds! My emeralds!"

She looked soft and vulnerable and my heart sort of melted.

"I'll take you down to the police station," I offered.

The girl from upstairs came down to see what all the commotion was about. We told her about the emeralds.

"My dear," she said, "*what* a palaver." There was a slight smile, very slight, in the curve of her lips. "You're insured, of course?"

Mary looked at her tearfully. She said nothing.

Then a thought seemed to occur to the other girl. Her hand went to her neck.

"My pearls," she said. "I'd better go upstairs and check they're safe." She came down in no time at all.

"They're gone," she said.

Sonny and I looked at each other in amazement. She had been in all morning.

"We're going to the police station," I said. "Would you like to come with us?"

"Oh no," she replied quickly. "I'll go with my husband when he gets back."

The cop shop in Brixton wasn't one of those places you visited lightly. There was a young pink-faced copper behind the counter, very tall, very cocky.

"Yes?"

Mary began explaining. Her English wasn't good at the best of times and her tears weren't making things any better.

"It would help, Madam, if you could speak English," the young copper told her.

I decided to intervene then. "This young lady has had her jewellery stolen," I explained.

"And who might you be?"

I recognised the accent, that tone of voice. The sort of voice that had so recently launched a thousand fires on the front line, the riots on Railton Road.

But I have to be fair to the young cop. I must explain that I looked terrifying those days with my wild locks, my wiry beard. (Bob Marley on a bad hair day.) Should that have mattered?

"And who might you be?" he asked. "Where were *you* at the time?"

I didn't deign to answer. I put my arm around Mary and gently propelled her out of the station. Pure white, perhaps, or even pure black might get you places. Brown got you nowhere.

The emeralds were never found.

《《《

Soon after that I kind of lost track of my neighbours, above and below. We moved site when work finished on the middle flat, though I continued living there a couple more months till it was sold. I was seeing a young West Indian mother then called Bhagwanti, who took me to wild Jamaican parties which began at two in the morning. Those days I survived on a staple of young mothers, so when anyone called me motherfucker it was a truly humbling experience.

I met Jesus on the stairs one Sunday morning.

"We're selling up," he said. "We've found ourselves a small cottage in Harrow."

"I'm really, really sorry," I answered. It was actually the best thing he could do, though I couldn't bring myself to tell him that. North London with its myriad shades of brown and brown was much more suited to their delicate needs.

"Don't be sorry," he said. "We've made a good profit on the flat and hopefully we'll be in the new place before the baby's born."

I wished him all the best and took his leave.

And the other couple, from the home counties?

I remember seeing them in Sainsbury's only a few days after the robbery. The good Doctor was trying to pull a pavlova out of the freezer cabinet and the wife was trying to restrain him.

"No Roger, no, no, no!" she was saying.

Oh, and she was wearing this rope of very fat, very juicy pearls around her neck.

Seedevi

"She has a seedevi face."
"I know, isn't it lovely?"
It's funny how they assume I can't speak English just because I'm in this cloth and jacket. Though to tell the truth, I don't actually speak it. But I understand it fairly well.

I was not always called Seedevi. When I was young, people who visited the house remarked on my features: serene, good-natured, fortunate. The face of someone who had read the Book of Life and understood thoroughly its contents. A lucky face. My parents began calling me Seedevi and it stuck. Seedevi by name, seedevi by nature, that's me. I suppose it may have been that in those early days I wasn't seedevi by nature, but I soon grew into the sort of behaviour my features so obviously expected of me, and I became good-natured and serene and benign.

I don't know what happened to the luck though. I married the man I loved, who I thought loved me.

My parents may have preferred someone of their own choosing but were good enough to acquiesce in my choice, and gave me the house in Pannipitiya as dowry. It was doubly bitter for me therefore when the abuse began, verbal as well as physical. You should have seen these seedevi features of a Saturday night when he came home drunk and hammered the life out of me. It was difficult for him I suppose after he lost his foot in the factory accident and couldn't get work any more. They bolted a block of hardwood six-by-five to the end of his leg and he clumped about on it all day; but you can only make so many excuses for people. You have no idea how much damage a piece of six-by-five can do to someone's face when they are lying helpless on the ground.

There were two teenage daughters by then. Their taciturn acceptance of things I could never understand, almost as if they condoned their father's behaviour. Not that they could have done anything about it, but a bit of moral support would have gone a long way.

So I walked out – in just the clothes I was wearing and a few bits and pieces in a siri-siri bag – leaving them the house and everything in it, everything I owned. I couldn't speak English, I didn't have much of a formal education. I had only ever cooked and cleaned for my thankless family – that is all I had been good for! – so that is what I became. But now I got paid for it, rather well too, and I could pick and choose who I worked for. I preferred Sri Lankan expatriates: those strange migratory birds in their colourful plumage, nostalgic for ethnic food yet foreign enough to treat you with the dignity you deserved: the dignity you never got from your own people.

When I walked through the doors of Westview I knew somehow this was it. Broken-down colonial, Mr. Perera called it, with its pillared portico, its pot-bellied fans. Beautiful, I called it. They were not your usual expats, the Pereras. They were not flashy and colourful and in-your-face. On the contrary they were quiet and middle-aged, like two overgrown mice really, in their matching grey outfits and their shrewd good-natured eyes. Funny how that colour grey does nothing for people of our hue: it drains the very life from our faces, giving us a washed-out sort of look.

More than the house I loved the garden, wild and bedraggled, with fruit trees and all sorts of palms, and large holes where the dogs had dug up the lawn.

So when they looked at each other and said, "She has a seedevi face," I knew I was in. It was then I told them:

"I have come here to die," I said. "If you're happy with me, I'll be here all my life." And if they were worried by that little declaration of faith they did not show it.

◇　◇　◇

I think they were happy with me. For them I curried the skins of the loofah, chopped fine in chilli and garlic; braised the roots of the lotus, in turmeric and coconut milk; fried the leaves of the murunga, crisp like seaweed; all those esoteric village dishes they were not likely to taste in other grand Cinnamon Gardens households. And all the while in my neat pink cloth and white jacket, slightly frilled at the neck in Galle lace, my *seedevi kit*.

Was I pretending, playing a part somehow, with this seedevi business? I like to think not, but you can't blame me, can you. I was only playing the system, you see.

Do you think I would have got the job if I'd turned up in cropped tee-shirt and flared pants as I so longed to do? No, I was the wise, all-knowing villager they would have me be. And if I was playing a role so were they: the well-meaning, very rich, slightly thick foreigners, all noble minds and deep pockets. Neither side understood the other very well and that was the key to our success: each was prepared to forgive the other its petty transgressions. We inhabited parallel but distinctly separate planes.

"Seedevi," Mrs. Perera said, "come on, I'll teach you English." But I knew the day I sat down with her I was doomed. This world, I have often thought, would be so much a better place if only we took the trouble to misunderstand our enemies a little, give them the benefit of our doubt. In my short life I have found it never does to look too closely into the minds of people: let their actions speak louder than their words. And their inactions loudest of all.

So it was a real eye-opener for me then when I died. I died one Saturday night while the Pereras were out dancing at the Supper Club. (Do mice dance?) My body struggled with the breathlessness of its enlarged lungs and I left it there on the floor after it had gasped its last, touching it solicitously one last time. I walked about that empty dark house a long time, all alone in my death.

Now those of you who think we others can fly about in an instant from place to place, think again: we are no more fleet of foot than you are in the real world. We cannot drive cars. We are dependent even more than you on public transport. The number of times I've had to use the 138 bus and curse its malodorous progress down the Havelock Road is not worth the telling.

"We must call the police!" said Mrs. Perera when they discovered the body. I nodded sagely behind them. If only I could use the telephone I would have dialled them myself. There is no force in my fingers though I feel as if I have the use of them; much as my husband still feels his toes even though the foot went a long time ago.

There was a small cop and big cop, a comedy duo, only without the comedy.

"Why is the body on the floor?" asked the small cop sternly. He had a baby face but he was the wicked one. (I could see into his mind, you see, I knew.)

"Seedevi always slept on the floor," said Mrs. Perera, "even though she had the bed. It was cooler."

"Why are all these doors and windows open?"

"They're never closed," said Mr. Perera gently. "There are too many in this house to close."

Then they saw the slight trickle of blood on the back of my white blouse.

"What's that?" asked the small cop aggressively. We all looked at it, mystified.

But the big cop had sharp eyes, bless his shapeless khaki cotton socks. There was a trail of ants leading all the way out to the balcony: the body was, literally, being eaten.

"There'll have to be a post-mortem," said the small cop with a little shiver of pleasure.

I slipped into the ambulance just as they were closing the doors. I always longed for one of those rides where they race through the city just like in films, cutting up traffic, crashing through red lights, scattering beggars and fruit carts with panache. And boy did I get it! My heart was quite palpitating by the time we got to the mortuary (my virtual heart that is; in reality I was quite heartless). All in all, one of the most exuberant days I ever spent, that day of my death; I heartily recommend the experience to each and every one of you at least once in your lifetime.

The Pereras and I sat on a wooden bench out in the open courtyard, surrounded on three sides by post-mortem rooms. We were in perfect harmony, no more misunderstanding; I understood them only too well now, a sad side-effect of death. Sadly boring, really. It was the time of the power cuts, there was no breeze and the stench was something appalling. I never knew I smelt so bad. I would have puked all over Mr. Perera's lovely stripey shirt if I'd had it in me, so to speak.

Halfway through they called him in. The body was on the slab, the skin on the face peeled back. There were two inches of blood and scum on the floor and the young blokes helping out were sloshing around in gumboots, happy as kids at the beach.

"For five thousand," they said, "we'll restore your mother beautifully. She'll look exactly like she did in real life."

But I had heard them talking inside the room. That face-peeling trick was one they employed all the time to get bereaving relations to cough up.

"That won't be necessary," said Mr. Perera.

Oh, I was so proud of him! That body in there had nothing to do with me. They could have hauled it off the slab and danced the baila with it for all I cared. I was prouder still he didn't deny it when they called me his mother.

It was sometime later that I heard it, the *klok, klok* of hardwood on asphalt. I could hear it a long way off in the still of that breathless afternoon, *klok, klok,* and I felt the sense of that approaching evil and was very thankful for once I was unseen.

"Murderer!" he screamed. "You killed her! You killed my beloved wife!"

But Mr. Perera sat there unmoved and I was blown away that someone so grey could be so brave. My husband sat down next to us on the bench and I could see there was murder on his mind.

"Where is it?" he kept asking, "Where is it, you bastard?"

But Mr. Perera sat there, his nose twitching with good-natured malice, secure in his lack of understanding.

The autopsy was done. The doctor called us over to her desk at the corner of the verandah. She pointed to Mr. Perera. "Because of the care of these people," she said to my husband, "your wife lived as long as she did. So I don't want to hear any more nonsense from you."

The comedy cops took Mr. Perera round the corner from the morgue to Nirvana Brothers, Undertakers.

"These are the people we recommend," they said. I knew they were getting a cut. Mr. Perera probably knew too, but he paid the fifteen thousand without comment and they took the body away, and we got the hell out of there.

But I hadn't seen the last of my family that day. They came to Westview to collect my belongings, with great protestations of love and grief. When they left I followed them up the road to the rubbish tip where they threw everything away, not having found what they came for. I can still see my pink skirt nestling coyly there among the rotting papaya skins and scavenging pariah dogs, seedevi to the bitter end.

Next day I rode to the funeral with the Pereras. Mr. P. turned to Mrs. P. "Funny Pitiya," he said, and I was mildly annoyed with him for being so facetious on so solemn an occasion.

Oh, you should have seen the people! The whole town had turned out. I was nothing to you then, I wanted to shout, what's changed? But as you can imagine I was speechless. All three political parties had sent representatives. The chief priest of the temple was making a speech and the Pereras were ushered to the front row next to my husband.

I slipped round the back to the kitchen to see what was cooking.

My daughters were in there. "She ought to be bloody grateful," said one, "all this trouble we're taking. All she ever did was walk out on us."

I could have died when she said that. Serves me right I suppose for eavesdropping.

I vaguely saw the body in the hall, all lipsticked up and tricked out in the coffin, but I passed on. It never does to look at yourself too closely when you're past your prime. (And I was, oh I was.) I wandered lonely in the crowds, among the old favourites: Siyadoris who couldn't wait for the petromaxes to be lit to get the dice out; those awful Silva children, bigger now but still uncontrollable. Emmy Akka, of course, ravishing in a sari of black net so appropriate to her recently attained widowhood. (No, I thought, *you* won't be going home alone tonight.)

"Where is it?" my husband was whispering to
Mr. Perera. "I know you have it."

But truly he had no idea. I had hidden it, you see.
In the bottom drawer of Mr. Perera's grey steel filing
cabinet, under the greyest of his grey London
correspondence. He never went in there, and
wouldn't know what it was even if he did: the deed to
this house, the Deed of Gift from my parents to me,
without which my family would never fully own it,
because their claim was defective, their ownership
incomplete. Not that it mattered one bit. They were
in possession and that's what really counts; but oh,
the moral victory was mine, however quixotic!

My eldest daughter was speaking to the crowd:
"Our mother was not just our mother, she was our
guide, our best friend. All we have here was hers, her
gift to us; the very proof, the embodiment of her
love."

In this world, you see, you must take the trouble
to build up your love on the solid rock of
misunderstanding, and give others the benefit of
your doubt. But I am no more of this world so I can
afford to stand back and laugh. Ha, if only I could!

The Pereras were ready to go. I slipped into the
car with them, and I don't know, it may have been the
humidity or even the excess of my emotion, but Mr.
Perera said, "It's awfully close in here, isn't it?" He put
the windows down and we drove back in silence all
the way home to Westview, and when we got there I
slipped upstairs to my room.

"I have come here to die," I told them. I never said anything about leaving, not even after death. This is my home now, this old house, I am in possession. I am the creak and groan of its rafters as they settle for the night in the great teakwood roof. I am the blur at the back of the black and white photograph hanging on the walls of the kitchen passage. That sudden matchstick flare of phosphorescence between the shifting plates of its time and space. Patina, character, call it what you will, it's not something money can buy or you can create easily. Unless you're prepared to wait a hundred years or so. But it comes for free when those like me move in.

And sometimes, when I'm at their end of the house in the early hours, and the million marghosa leaves on the tree outside, backlit by the moon, shiver against the bottle-glass of the windows causing a strange luminescence, then he thinks he hears me banging about and I know he longs to call out:

"Seedevi, you know last week how you cooked that fantastic karavila? Do you think we might have the same again today, please?"

But he doesn't. He wakes up and goes off for his run in those absurdly long shorts of his and that comical headband, almost safe in the satisfaction that when he comes back I'll be there to greet him with his morning coffee, and say:

"If you go to Raheema's this morning and get me just half a pound, and maybe some garlic and ginger, I'll make it for you just the way I did that other day."

But Did I Tell You I Can't Dance ?

Ihad made my preparations early. The night
before, I polished my shoes – handmade and
English – and blue-blacked my hair, thankfully still
my own. At my age it's all about the hair, as George
Clooney once said. I left the flat in Princess Court
with a last look in a passing mirror and blew myself a
kiss.

"Knock 'em dead, bitch," I said.

It was all go at the Widows Friendly Society
when I got there. I drove the aged limo round the
back and parked between a grazing cow and a silver
Hiace van, out of which they were decanting a
woman with silver hair, into a silver wheelchair, all
properly colour coordinated. There were masses of
young people, every one of them in their mid-
twenties, and here was I very much on the wrong side
of fifty, though that is strictly between you and me
and the pages of this book, you understand. I will
only ever admit to forty-nine, and that after a couple
of strong arrack-and-sodas.

I held up my chin and walked straight in. Inside was a man young as the rest but with all the cares of the world resting on his weary brow: the instructor. He gave me a form to fill. It was basic and so were my answers:

Name: Brian de Kretser II

Age: Never you mind

Sex: Not as often as I should like

Address: 22 Princess Court, Cinnamon Gardens, Colombo 7

"Gents to the left of me, ladies to the right," shouted the instructor, "let's go, people!" With a practised flick of the wrist he activated the music machine, and off we went.

You know how in films you see the hero in his raft poised at the top of the rapids? And then in a split second he's over the edge and all you see are bits of orange raft and thrashing limbs and the foamy white roar of the water? Well that is how I felt. All around me there were limbs moving to the roar of the music, moving in unison like a mighty wave of water. And there was I in the middle of all this, and in my heart, silence. I was hopelessly out of my depth. You may have gathered by now this was my first dance class, but did I tell you I can't dance?

It all began the week before, New Year's Day to be precise, at the bar of the Capri Club where I meet up once a week with my buddies: all men of a certain age, with increasing bank balances and receding hairlines, impressive cv's and depressive ex-wives. Cholesterol, high blood pressure, varicose veins, you name it we have it. Not that we admit to any of this in each other's company, you understand, we are all such superstars.

Have you ever had a wicked-looking red sports car pull up next to you at the traffic lights and you think, wow! and you look closer and there's this wrinkled fruit sitting inside with a baseball cap on backwards, and you go, oh, what a waste! Well you know what? That's probably me in there or one of my mates.

Anyway to get back to the story, there we were that day and the talk was as usual about the lack of decent girls in this town.

"What about the Russians? What about the karaoke girls?" asked Pujitha, who was in an argumentative mood.

"We know all about your White Russians!" I snapped. "When I mean decent, I mean decent: someone who'll be happy to come out with you, and not expect anything in return."

"No such person."

"Yes, well I'm forced to agree," I said sadly.

Then my friend Athula spoke up, quiet dark horse that he is. "Has anybody been to the WFS on a Sunday morning?"

"WFS?"

"The Widows Friendly Society."

"Don't talk to me about friendly widows," I began, but they all shut me up.

"Every Sunday morning," Athula continued, "you see the most gorgeous girls streaming out of the WFS. They come there for the ballroom dancing classes. I think it's high time we joined up," he said, looking smug.

But as it happened I was the only one who did, the others having chickened out at the last minute: one had to take his aged mother to get her corns cut, another was doing a fasting-blood-sugar test; the third was off to Rani Fernando Salons for his weekly facial. The only truth about men of a certain age is that the older they get the more cowardly they become....

"Now each of you select a partner," shouted the instructor just when I thought it couldn't get any worse. This is the point where the professional dancers go for each other with little self-satisfied smirks on their faces, and the rest of us are left to wonder, will I get the good-natured one with the thunder thighs, or the coy one with the furry armpits, or the anorexic in the day-glo socks? Well, I couldn't believe my eyes. This girl was all elbow and leg, quite one of the most beautiful things you ever saw; and when you're like me, in between your second and third wife, believe me you've seen a lot. I always think that that length of arm between collar-bone and elbow-tip is the real give-away, and this girl had arms all the way to Jaffna.

"Hello Uncle," she said.

I had to decide quickly whether to bristle or not. At my age you get plenty of opportunities, but let me tell you, bristling is bad for business.

So instead I smiled sweetly and said: "Hello there yourself, beautiful!"

She smiled back in an abstracted sort of way, and for a while both of us concentrated on the main business of the day, the fancy footwork. It soon became obvious we were both quite hopeless.

"And now," said the instructor, "I will teach you the basic steps, the rudiments merely, of the jive."

For those of you not in the know, this is a particularly graceless dance where you have to step to the left and step to the right, like a geriatric horse with a bit of ginger up its arse. The music is equally jerky and raucous. I thought Beauty and I were making quite a spirited go of things when there was a commotion at the other end of the hall and the music stopped. The crowd parted like the waves of the Red Sea and a silvery two-wheeler shot through, hissing and squeaking to a halt in front of the two of us.

"No, no, no! Don't you realise this is a happy, happy, dance, so look happy, for God's sake!" We were too stunned to reply.

"What's wrong with you, Uncle?" continued the woman with the silvery hair, "You're hopeless at this aren't you?"

"Well Auntie, you can't be much better in that thing, can you?" I shot back. As you have gathered by now, political correctness is not my strong suit.

There was a shocked silence in the room, apart from the slight sighing of the wheelchair.

Then a low cackle. "You're good!" she said, "You're good, but I'm better! By the way, I'm not your Auntie, never was, never will be. Everyone here calls me Ama. I'm the one who runs this class."

That was my first introduction to Ama, the beginning for me of a new epoch.

"This is my son Sanjay," she continued, "the useless good-for-nothing. If it wasn't for me, this class would fold up." The instructor her son looked at me over the top of her head. I couldn't quite fathom the expression on his face.

At the end of the class Ama wheeled herself up to me again.

"You know I was the All-Island Ballroom Dancing Champion of 1962?"

"Yes," I said, "I can see."

Her eyes narrowed for a minute wondering whether I was making fun of her. Then she laughed again, a sort of gargle at the back of her throat.

"Now what I want you to do is this," she continued. "I want you to find Sanjay a nice young girl. He'll never find one here, you see, among all this riff-raff."

It was unfortunate for her the room went quiet just then. Her words went down a treat I can tell you among all those bright young things.

At this point I did the decent thing, the only thing possible.

"I think Sanjay should meet my partner," I said.

I turned to her. "I never did catch your name, my dear."

"Sarita," she replied.

"Sanjay, meet Sarita. Sarita, Sanjay."

Easy as that. They looked at each other a full two seconds, and let me tell you in this business a full two seconds is a long, long time. It cut my heart to bits.

His need was probably greater than mine, and anyway, who's to say she'd have had me? In matters like these I have always been the perfect gentleman; maybe now you understand why my second wife ran off with my best friend. But that is another story.

I gave Sarita a lift home in the old limo.

"Do you mind if I smoke?" she asked.

"Not at all, go right ahead."

She looked thoughtfully around the leather-lined interior. "Who was your last passenger, Uncle, Abraham Lincoln?"

"You don't have to call me Uncle, you know. My name is Brian."

"OK, Brian." A slight smile hovered in the curl of her lips.

I drove her to Nugegoda where she lived, in a little self-contained annexe.

"Will you come in for a coffee?" she asked.

"Won't your parents mind?"

"I live alone. Anyway it'll give the landlord something to talk about."

I don't know what possessed me, but I asked: "Weren't you being a bit bold back there, accepting a lift from someone you'd only just met in a dance class?"

"Oh it's OK, Uncle, I knew I could trust you."

Just the words I didn't want to hear. We parked the limo in the drive of a well-tended garden and went inside. There were two iron-and-rexine Arpico armchairs from the Sixties under a neon light. A small TV stood in the corner and above it a lone calendar on a nail.

"It came furnished," she said by way of explanation.

I don't know about you but I always feel sad when I see the inside of anyone's house: people seem to hold so much mystery and promise when you meet them first; then you see them in their natural habitat and they are diminished somehow, lessened; and you wonder, perhaps, how someone so exquisite can flourish somewhere so mundane. And you think, why is it that people with real poetry in their hearts seem able to carry it about with them sublimely unaware of the banality of their surroundings? Now me, I have fine furniture and paintings, bone china and cut glass all around me. It must mean I have absolutely nothing inside.

"So what are you doing Tuesday night?" I asked.

"Nothing."

"Good, then you're coming out to dinner with me."

She didn't make a fuss like your normal Sri Lankan girl. But then she can't have been entirely normal to want to go out with me. Maybe she wasn't entirely Sri Lankan either.

ଚ୍ଚ ଚ୍ଚ ଚ୍ଚ

I took her to the Gallery Café. There is always an air of Tibetan calm about that place, with water lilies floating in pools, and disembodied voices, fragrant like incense in the air. Shanth the owner came out to greet us, dapper as ever in full black.

"I didn't know you had such a beautiful daughter?"

"Nor did I. This is my niece," I said looking at Sarita meaningfully. "I'm her Uncle," I explained further, to dispel any lingering doubts there may have been.

We were shown to a table in the ochre courtyard.

"So tell me about yourself."

"What's to tell?" she asked gloomily. "Oh, I see, you want to know why I'm here, single, living on my own. It's funny how I get asked that question all the time. As if single girls in Sri Lanka don't have the right to live on their own."

"Well it is rather unusual out here, a girl of your age entirely on her own. Don't you have parents, aunts, uncles, who worry for your safety?"

"One aunt," she replied, "who has three children of her own and was hell to live with. I was with her a month when I first came back. She thought I was a bad influence on my cousins, so I moved out. Actually, I had only planned on being there temporarily, till I found my bearings.

Anyway, why should anyone worry for my safety here?" she continued fiercely. "It's a hell of a lot safer than London or New York."

"And parents?"

"My English father died last year."

"I'm really sorry." I tried to take her hand but she withdrew it. At that moment I could see she wasn't with me, she was somewhere far away, in another place.

"My mother's Sri Lankan. She can't stand it here. She thinks it's the arsehole of the world."

"So she just passed through," I added.

Sarita gave a hoot of laughter that had other diners looking up. We ordered our food: Thai vegetables with jasmine rice for me because us superstars have to watch our waistlines. I watched wistfully while she put away half a chicken.

"Anyway, she's very happy for me to be back here," Sarita continued. "She thought I was wasting my time in London."

"And she wants you to find a nice Sri Lankan husband."

"Funny you say that. It's exactly what she said."

"Does that, by any chance, include anyone over fifty?"

She looked at me thoughtfully for a moment.

"I don't think so," she said quietly.

Now my Philosophy of Life has always been, if at first you don't succeed, give up and go home.

This time I felt it might be worth breaking the rules, worth persevering. So I hung on in there.

Shanth came and sat with us for a moment.

"How's business?" I asked.

"Oh not bad, not bad at all. The other day the prime ministers of India and Sri Lanka walked in, completely unannounced."

"And you managed to find them a table, surprising even yourself," I added. He shot me a look and continued on his rounds.

Sarita pushed back her plate with a satisfied sigh. "That was really, really good. It's not often I get taken out," she said, "and never to a place like this."

"Pudding?" She shook her head.

"How about some coffee?"

"It keeps me awake at night."

"You're made to be kept awake at night," I said softly as we got up to go.

ℜ ℜ ℜ

I told my mates at the Capri all about Ama and Sanjay, omitting any mention of Sarita: even the fact of knowing her seemed somehow too good to be shared. I don't remember much about that evening except that I ended it out in the Capri garden on top of a wooden table, showing my friends the basic steps, the *rudiments* merely, of the jive, under a sickly moon and a tall tree well-hung with bats.

Next Sunday she greeted me with her usual abstracted air.

"How was the rest of your week, Uncle?"

"So much the worse for not having seen you."

Silence.

We continued with our geriatric horse dance. At the interval Sanjay came up to us.

"Ama wants you to come and have lunch with us next Saturday. Are you free?"

"I'm free," I said in my best *Are-you-being-served* voice. I wrote down their address, somewhere off the Havelock Road. "Anyway, where is she today?"

"Oh, Ama isn't feeling too well today." He paused. "It's a shame, because I was planning to go down south this afternoon."

"So what's to stop you?"

He looked helpless. "I can't leave her on her own."

"Isn't there anyone else in the house?"

"There's old Kamala, of course, to look after her, but she needs me around. Otherwise she feels awfully depressed."

"What actually is wrong, if you don't mind me asking, for her to be in a wheelchair?"

"You know Ama, she can never sit still even when she's doing something. She was wandering round the house brushing her teeth, and tripped over the step into the bathroom. She fractured a small bone in her foot and had to be in a wheelchair for a while. Now the bone's healed but she can't walk anymore. The doctors can't understand it. I think she was too nervous to use the leg originally and now she's lost the use of it." He shrugged. "I've taken her to loads of doctors. One even went so far as to say she was shamming." He grinned. "She gave him such a bollocking, I think he had to take a panadol and lie down at the end of that consultation."

"Does she always feel unwell before one of your trips?" I asked curiously.

There was a flicker of grim humour in his eyes. "Yes," he said and turned away. It occurred to me then that he hadn't invited Sarita. At the end of the lesson it became clear why.

"Shall I drop you home?" I asked. She shook her head.

"I'm going with Sanjay."

So they had made prior arrangements. I was, it seems, already out of the picture.

ಬ   ಬ   ಬ

Sanjay and Ama lived in a small bungalow in a cul-de-sac off the Havelock Road. There was an air of neglect about the front garden. The gate was open and I walked up to the front door. There was no bell anywhere so I rapped on the door with my key. Silence. I could hear the faint rumble of traffic far away on Havelock Road. I rapped again.

"Hello! Is there anyone there?" I called out.

"Coming! I'm coming, for God's sake," said an irate voice. There was a fumbling and scratching from inside and the door swung open to reveal Ama in her wheelchair.

"You old people, you have no patience," she said.

"Good morning, oh spring chicken! Kindly move your vehicle out of the way so I can come in." I followed her into a small sitting room with polished cement floors.

"Sanjay and Sarita have gone out to get some booze," she said.

I felt cold, as if someone had left the door open to my heart and let the draught in. But I recovered quickly. Us old timers do.

"They needn't have bothered," I said. "I brought a bottle of rum and a bottle of Passiona to make you my rum punch. It's quite famous in Colombo. I just need you to squeeze some limes."

"Come into the kitchen, then."

I followed her down a long dimly-lit passage hung with black and white photographs in wooden frames, all of Ama.

"From my dancing days," she explained.

We went into a neat kitchen, with formica cupboards chipped here and there but generally in very good condition.

"You know, you keep this place very well," I said, "considering.."

"Considering I'm stuck in this thing? I spend all day cleaning. Kamala comes in every day to give a hand, but I have to be behind her. And Sanjay is absolutely hopeless. He has no idea what running a house involves. He doesn't know the meaning of the word cleaning, and he thinks meals appear as if by magic."

"Well, you brought him up."

"Don't I know it! My husband used to say, you spoil him, you live with the consequences. Mind you, he was a wicked, wicked man, my husband. He died leaving me with all these debts and a child to bring up. That's when I took up dancing. Can you imagine, Chevalier D'Almeida's daughter having to give dancing classes?"

I looked at her. She was a ruin, but a magnificent ruin: Sigiriya perhaps, or the Brazen Palace. She must have been absolutely striking in her day when she was on her feet.

"Ama, if only you were ten years younger and I was ten years older, you wouldn't be safe alone in this room with me."

"But you *are* ten years older."

There was no answer to that so we continued squeezing limes in silence. After a while she said, "This girl you've introduced Sanjay to, she's totally unsuitable."

"So, it's my fault, now, is it?"

"I didn't say that. But she has a stubborn streak in her. I can see it in her eyes."

"Ha! So she refuses to do what you say!"

"On the contrary, she does exactly as I say. But I know what she's thinking. It's your turn now, Ama, but just you wait till we're married. It'll be my turn then."

"And what's wrong with that? You know Ama, you can't keep that boy under your thumb for ever. You have to resign at some point, let the new boss take over!　But what makes you so sure they're serious? They've only just met."

"They've been together every damned day since he took her out to dinner last week."

I felt a little pinprick of jealousy. "Where did they go?"

"McDonalds, KFC, I don't know. Why?"

I thought to myself, it didn't need a meal at the Gallery. All it took was the price of a hamburger. A mean thought, and I suppressed it.

"Anyway," Ama was saying, "I know that type. They're only after money."

I was beginning to get annoyed with her. "So, that's okay then. You've already told me you don't have any, so you're quite safe."

"What little I have," she said ignoring my sarcasm, "will all be left to Tibbles, if anything like that happens."

"Tibbles?"

She pointed to a furry heap on top of the fridge which opened one malevolent yellow eye, looked at me, and closed it again. It looked very like the hair-piece Pujitha had thrown out just last week after being teased mercilessly by the rest of us at the Capri Club.

"And is Tibbles going to look after you in your old age?"

"No, but the nuns will. The nuns who run the WFS also run a wonderful old people's home. They won't forget I'm Chevalier D'Almeida's daughter when the time comes."

"What's all this about nuns?" asked Sanjay coming into the kitchen. Sarita followed him in, rather sheepishly I thought.

"Never you mind. Let's see what you've got there."

Sanjay put down a plastic bag on the kitchen table and pulled out a bottle of Arrack.

"Very Special Old Piss," said Ama. (Sarita and I looked at each other in disbelief.) "I thought I told you to get whisky?"

"I would have, if you'd given me enough money. Anyway, who are you trying to impress?"

Ama looked at me.

"Oh I drink anything," I said quickly, "as long as it's wet."

I poured them rum punch and we sat round the kitchen table.

"Ama is treating us to her seafood buryani," said Sanjay. "She only cooks it for special people."

Ama looked pleased at this. Then a disquieting thought seemed to cloud her face. She turned to Sarita. "Tell me my dear, for the life of me I can't place who's who you are. Are you, by any chance, related to the Diases of Panadura?" Sarita shook her head. "I don't think so. But I may well be related to the Veddahs of Bibile."

Ama's brow blackened. She could have taken a crack like that from me, maybe, but not from a prospective daughter-in-law.

Sanjay cut in quickly. "I think it's time Brian told us something about himself."

"Well you know the old story," I began, "the one that goes, My father wasn't rich but my uncle had piles? Well in this case father was rich, and he died, leaving it all to little ol' me."

"But what do you do?" Ama asked.

"Nothing really," I replied truthfully. "I'll never forget the sign my father had in his office, 'If you have nothing to do, don't do it here.' In my case I do nothing, but I do it beautifully. My whole life, I feel, is a work of art."

"But don't you feel duty bound, don't you feel you owe it, to help others?" I could feel Ama's Catholic moral indignation welling up.

"Frankly, no. I'm not a Buddhist but I feel they've got it just right when they say, do no harm to others, live a peaceful life, be kind. It's a lot better than blundering about trying to do good. If you think the less fortunate are grateful to you, you're sadly mistaken. You only end up earning their everlasting resentment."

"Oh, you wicked, wicked man," breathed Ama.

I left them that afternoon feeling a little sorry. Sorry for myself because I was ageing and alone and

no party to that strange little family unit that was
beginning to form; sorry for them because they were
really three quite disparate elements, oil, water and
vinegar, and there was a lot of shaking up to do
before they could form anything even remotely
cohesive.

ക   ക   ക

Next class there was no sign of Sarita, and I got the
girl with the day-glo socks. Lucky, lucky me.

"What do you do when you're not here?" she
asked, eyes half-closed, concentrating on the serious
business of chewing gum.

"I'm unemployed, so not an awful lot."

"I swim a lot," she confided, blowing a bubble in
my face.

She twiddled me around effortlessly.

"Hey, aren't I supposed to be the one doing the
leading?"

"Well, somebody's got to do it," she said
cryptically. I smiled benevolently and let myself be
led around, thinking of my ex-wives who had pretty
much done the same, cursing Sarita for not being
there.

At the end of the class she said, "Hey, maybe we
could go swimming sometime? Maybe this
afternoon?"

" 'Fraid not," I replied, "I've got my period."

Outside under the banana trees I was reversing
the car when my way was blocked by the familiar

silver two-wheeler. Ama signalled to me to put the window down.

"Where's Sarita?" she asked.

"Shouldn't I be the one asking you?"

"You don't think they had a fight?"

"How should I know? Why?" I asked, beginning to get suspicious, "Did you provoke one?"

"No," she replied, looking guilty as hell.

"Look Ama," I said, getting a little exasperated, "do you want Sanjay to get married or not? How do you think he's ever going to get to know anyone if you keep putting them off? How many others have you done this to?"

There was a pause. "One, maybe two… they were really much worse than Sarita."

"So you mean Sarita is quite suitable in comparison?"

"Hey, let's not get carried away here. She has her points."

"Well I think you've gone quite far enough. Please try to keep that troublesome mouth of yours under control in future. And now, kindly give way to a superior vehicle."   I negotiated around her wheelchair and drove off.

Back home I had just got my dancing shoes off when the phone rang. Sarita.

"What are your shopping skills like?" she asked.

"Brilliant. Why didn't you come to class?" I riposted.

"I've got to buy a shirt for Sanjay. Help me choose. Meet me at Odel in an hour."

Odel was packed when I got there. I was early. (Why is it the old are always early, the young always late?) I strolled up and down the aisles followed at a discreet six paces by the young, fresh-faced staff. Do I have an untrustworthy sort of look? I guess I do because I'm always followed. Many a time I've wanted to turn round suddenly and go boo! but I've never dared. They'd probably collapse in a heap and burst into tears.

"I'm looking for shorts," I told my young followers just to get rid of them.

They showed me a purple silky thing, the size of a small parachute.

"I could always jump out of a plane in that," I said. "Then again, I'd probably have to, if anybody saw me wearing those around Colombo."

"They're made for the American market," they said proudly.

"So I see," I replied.

Sarita blew in half an hour late, clattering through the gents department awkwardly elegant in grey and white. "Have you eaten?"

"Yes," I lied. (The truth is, us superstars never, hardly ever, eat unless we have to, saving up our calories for those special occasions.) She began rifling through the racks.

"Ama buys all his clothes," she said. "They're all so fuddy-duddy. Time for a change."

"How are things over there?" I asked, a little disingenuously.

"She's so mean to me, you can't believe."

"Oh, I certainly can."

"And the worst thing, Sanjay actually puts up with it. He lets her say all those horrible things. By not answering back it's almost as if he's agreeing with her."

"Well you know you have another option, don't you? Leave him. Come to me."

"Don't be silly, I'm in love with him."

There it was then: the axe on the block, the severed fingers bloodied and twitching on the side. But us veterans are trained to ignore the blood. I stood there without flinching.

"Sarita, what exactly are you looking for in life?"

She gave me her bitter sweet smile, one I had come to grow quite familiar with.

"If I knew that, Uncle, I wouldn't be here with you now, would I?"

I looked at her then and couldn't help comparing the two of us: I who had been everywhere, knew nothing; she who had been nowhere but still seemed to know so much more. I felt an inexpressible sadness. For her or me I couldn't tell.

"Why can't he walk out? Why does he have to be tied to her apron strings?"

"Sarita," I said, "listen to me. Who would look after her if he walked out? This is not the sort of country where an old person can manage easily on their own, let alone someone in a wheelchair. There are no old age benefits, no golden years, no golden sunsets. It all gets rather black towards the end."

"And I'm supposed to suffer on that count," she said bitterly.

"All I can say is you're not the only one. Listen, Sri Lanka has the fastest ageing population in recorded history. Did you know that? In a few years there'll be many more of us than there'll be of you. Get used to it."

"My, we are being candid today," she replied. But sarcasm didn't suit her; really, she was too beautiful for that.

"Just give as good as you get," I said, "and she'll back down." I didn't tell her then what Ama had told me in the car park. That might have given her too much hope.

She chose an improbably loud shirt, with purple and green stripes.

"That is not going to be popular with Ama," I warned.

"In that case I won't insist on her wearing it."

ℛ ℛ ℛ

January came to an end and with it the waltz and jive. At the start of February we progressed to the rhumba and cha-cha.

There are certain days in a single man's calendar, black-letter days you wish could be obliterated entirely. Christmas is one: people invite you round because it's their last good deed of the year. They're extra nice because being single in Colombo is seen as an even bigger handicap than being in a wheelchair: they feed you up on yellow rice and chicken curry, and give you too much arrack to drink till you end up being quietly sick in the downstairs lavatory. Valentine's Day is another, though on this particular day there are never any invitations. I had agreed to meet up with the other superstars at the Capri, but when Sanjay rang I was secretly pleased.

"February 14th is Ama's birthday," he said.

"It's also Valentine's Day," I pointed out. "Aren't you taking Sarita out somewhere?"

"I had planned to." There was a pause. "But how can I leave Ama alone on a day like that? Anyway she usually likes to have people round. She'd like you to come."

"Have you at least bought Sarita a gift?"

"I bought her a ring."

Now take it from me that's a dangerous sort of gift to give a woman. Wife number one had cornered me after just such an episode.

"Sanjay, do you know what you're doing?"

"Yes. At least I think so. Anyway," he added softly, "only time will tell."

੨੭ ੨੭ ੨੭

Someone had hung a red paper lantern in the overgrown garden giving the place an air of grim festivity, like one of those Korean brothels which were just then springing up all over Colpetty.

In the tropic gloom I could make out a figure seated on the verandah steps. There was a bottle of arrack by his side, three-quarters full.

"Top of the morning to you," he said.

I smiled politely and went inside. There was no one in the sitting room and I walked through to the kitchen. Sarita, Sanjay and Ama were all seated on one side of the kitchen table like strangers waiting for a train. Sanjay's purple and green shirt spoke loud enough for the three of them. The furry hairpiece was in its usual place on top of the fridge. The atmosphere was thick, and not just from the cigarette smoke.

"Sanjay always buys me something in gold," Ama was saying, "something small, usually, a pendant or brooch or ring. I can't think what got into him this year. He knows I have enough and more saris."

Sarita didn't say anything. She was playing with a little maroon velvet box, opening and shutting it. Inside was a ring. In silver.

"What's with the bloke outside?" I asked.

Sarita looked up. "That's Sanjay's Uncle Gerard. Don't mind him."

"Happy birthday Ama," I said, pushing across my present.

"Oh, another sari, how *nice!* As I was saying it's really quiet this year, everyone very busy, people had other plans, all except Gerard."

She turned to me. "I tried to force Sanjay to take Sarita out somewhere but he insisted, absolutely insisted, lovely boy, he'd stay at home and keep his old mother company on her birthday."

"The lovely boy," echoed Sarita. She looked at me but I looked away, unwilling to be party to any confidences. Indeed, there were strange truths floating around the room that night like flies around a Bombay duck, landing unwanted on each of us, brushed away by each of us in turn. Ama continued her monologue.

"Hopeless, absolutely hopeless. Can't look after himself, can't even choose his own clothes. I don't know how he'll manage when I'm gone..."

"Bollocks," muttered Sanjay, "you know damn well it's me looking after you, not the other way round."

"....can't even look after Tibbles..."

"Fuck Tibbles," said Sanjay.

Sarita giggled and I sat there speechless, wondering what they'd put in the drink.

"That's why I have to be here. Keep an eye on him. Protect him from fortune hunters..."

"Ama," said Sarita, with quiet venom in her voice. "You bitch."

There was a sudden squeak of pain from the wheelchair.

And Ama stood up!

Our three jaws dropped in unison.

"That's it!" she screamed, "Either she goes, or I go!"

We watched horrified and fascinated as Ama loomed over us, swaying slightly, a serpent uncoiled from its basket.

Then she sat back down again and the spell was broken.

"So that's that then." Sanjay looked bleakly from one woman to the other.

I got up in my turn. "Ama, I think you're way out of line here." A weak defence, too little, too late, the story of my life.

"Shut up, you old roué," she said calmly, "this is strictly between me and my son."

Then I said the words I'd been meaning to for a very long time:

"Ama, you wicked, wicked woman."

Outside, the motionless figure sat under the paper globe, red like the rising sun. The bottle of arrack stood by his side, three-quarters empty.

"Top of the morning to you too," I said as I left.

ം ം ം

A light rain was falling as I parked the old limo and got out. I noticed the drive was freshly gravelled and bordered by dwarf ixoras. Inside I was shown into a small sitting room smelling of tea leaves and wax polish.

"I'll see whether she's free to see you," said the plump young nun with a smile. "As you know, she's not at home to everybody." Moments later the familiar hiss and squeak in the corridor and Ama wheeled herself in.

"Ama! Are they looking after you all right?"

"Of course," she replied. And truly, she looked radiant. "The nuns are extremely good to me. Well they could hardly fail to be, could they, once they realised I was Chevalier D'Almeida's daughter? And the best part," she continued, "I get to keep Tibbles."

I noticed the hairy heap on her lap.

"They've even promised to look after him once I'm gone."

"Oh Ama, don't be so morbid. You'll outlive us all, I'm sure." Then I came to the point of my visit. "I have a message from Sanjay and Sarita. Will you come and spend the day with them now you're more settled? They'll come and fetch you, and we can all have lunch together just like old times."

"Absolutely not!" She sounded genuinely shocked and if I didn't know her better I would have been convinced. "My dear Brian, these young ones need a chance to grow up and develop in their own way. They have to make their own mistakes you know. No amount of us telling will help. Us old people have a duty to keep away! That means you too, by the way."

I laughed, a little uncomfortably. Me! Old!

"So no, I don't think I'll visit them just yet. I don't want to be poking my nose where I'm not needed. The moment I realised they were right for each other, I knew it was my duty to move out. So let them get on with it, and good luck to them, I say."

Just like Ama, I thought. Having painted herself into a corner, here she was, brandishing the paintbrush, whooping and hollering. If all old people were as feisty as her, maybe this place wouldn't be half as bad in time to come.

As I reversed the car on my way out I thought I would go and see her as often as I could.

She was genuinely glad to see me, and in truth there were lessons to be learnt: she was, if I could bear to admit it to myself, only just that little bit further down the road than I was.

As for Tibbles, he has treated me throughout with all the condescension I doubtless deserve. I understand. He will, after all, be one day a very rich cat.

Fidel Sent The Plane

"I wonder if you remember us from the old days? Friends of your grandfather's, here in London till the end of the week. We should love to see you, nine o'clock sharp, Thursday morning.... I'm rather afraid this time we're having to slum it at the Park Lane Hilton – there are too many of us in the Presidential party to be accommodated elsewhere!"

The note left out far more than it said. It didn't refer for instance to that previous missive – which Asela's father had shown him – outlining the dowry, on three pages of watery blue Claridge's notepaper.

Asela slipped it furtively into the pocket of his rather ancient suit while Jamelia watched luxuriously from the bed.

"My, we are looking smart this morning!" She worked in a small charity shop on the High Street and didn't have to go in till ten. Some days, if the toast got burnt or she broke a heel, she didn't bother to go in at all.

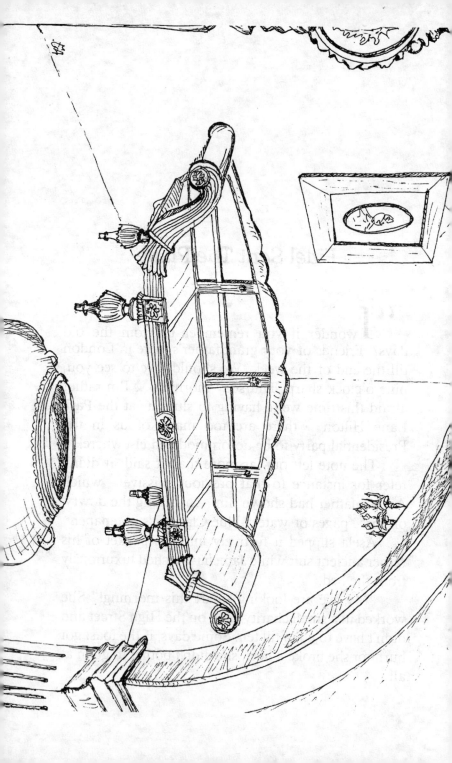

"Appointment with the bank manager," Asela said. He bent over and bit her on the lip. "Be back early," he whispered.

He had taken the day off work, he didn't have to report to the site. He left the flat, crossed the concrete walkway and down the steps, past the huge metal bins at the bottom which were big enough to accommodate human bodies. And sometimes did.

Outside on Upper Richmond Road the rain fell solidly, efficiently. For his luck a bus arrived as soon as he got to the stop and he even found a seat. He settled back to do what he always did best: to dream: What am I? Who am I?

The entire eighth floor of the Hilton was taken over by the Sri Lankan party. There were people milling in corners, discreet and important on the deep-pile green carpet.

Somewhere, Asela thought, in the beating heart of Colombo – Narahenpita? Kirilapone? – there must be a secret school where they taught you Discreet and Important. Most of those present were Graduates, Class Two. The chef-de-cabinet was all the way at one end in a suite. Class One, with Distinction.

Asela knocked and waited.

The door was opened after a while by an aged and angular Kumarihamy.

"One of the many, many disadvantages of London," she complained. "Nobody to open your door."

She was resplendent in a sari of shot silk, red and green, which changed colour as she walked. She looked like a sort of wayward, postmodern traffic light, flashing and ambulant. A bit early in the morning for silk, Asela thought, as he followed her into a magnificent room overlooking Hyde Park, an endless carpet beyond the green of the room. Through an open doorway he could see the chef-de-cabinet in a sarong, seated on the edge of the bed, packing what looked like chocolates into a large porcelain jar.

"We were just wrapping up the Commonwealth Conference in the Bahamas," she was saying, "when Fidel sent us the plane. Can you imagine? Just H.E. and us for lunch. And moments before we flew back he presented us with five glorious jars, filled to the brim with chocolates!

"Now tell me about yourself."

Not much to tell, Asela thought.

"We've known your family for generations of course, from the Malabar Street days. But you grew up in that little street, didn't you, off the Peradeniya Road?"

Those were only almshouses, Asela wanted to say, that my great-grandfather built to take up the overflow, when there were too many Nayakes in Malabar Street.

We grew up on the opposite side, on the hill. By then the King was long gone so you could build above the level of his palace. Before that, as you know, you had to have permission for roof tiles, rank for finials. And we had both.

But Asela refrained. He was here at a job interview, a job for life he didn't even want, and the cardinal rule for a job applicant is that he must not boast. And anyway, all this talk of finials didn't sit at all easily with the concrete council flat in Putney, or the labourer's job in Brixton, or the luscious secret that was Jamelia.

Who am I? What am I?

The Kumarihamy was talking and Asela was mesmerized by the alexandrite on her finger, that matched her outfit – splashing colours as she moved her hand this way and that – alternately encouraging and repelling, green, red, green.

"We'll write to your father when we get home. We'll let him know."

She got to her feet and Asela followed in a daze. So was it red for stop, then, or green for go? He didn't know but as he left, it struck him painfully how she hadn't even thought to offer one of those *glorious* chocolates Fidel so kindly sent over on the plane.

And back home that night in bed he shed a single tear for himself, into the wiry brown mass that was Jamelia's hair, thinking for what must have been the hundredth time, What am I? Who am I?